DON GIOVANNA

STRANGE LOOP
THE CABALIST
CONVERSATIONS WITH LORD BYRON
ON PERVERSION, 163 YEARS AFTER
HIS LORDSHIP'S DEATH
THE SIDE OF THE MOON
PROTO ZOË
THE YOUNG ITALIANS
THE KINGDOM OF FANES
ZOË TROPE
LETTER TO LORENZO

DON GIOVANNA

AMANDA PRANTERA

BLOOMSBURY

First published 2000

Copyright © 2000 by Amanda Prantera

The moral right of the author has been asserted

Bloomsbury Publishing, 38 Soho Square, London WIV 5DF

A CIP catalogue record for this book
is available from the British Library

ISBN 0 7475 4927 3

10 9 8 7 6 5 4 3 2

Typeset by Hewer Text Ltd, Edinburgh
Printed in Great Britain by Clays Ltd, St Ives plc

To my father Nicky Morriss

'We come into this world,
We lodge and we depart.
He never dies
That's lodged within my heart.'

DON GIOVANNA

Light-hearted drama in practically no acts at all

Cast in order of appearance:

Lord **HENRY** Thirsk .... Baritone
JOANNA Volpi... Mezzo soprano
Lady Henry (**GAIA**) Thirsk .... Soprano
AMABILE Bucci .... Mezzo soprano
ORSO Maria Volpi .... Bass
Florence Rossi d'Avola.. Soprano
Emily Parker .... Soprano
Isobel Marcucci.. Soprano
Journalist.. Alto
Louise Shapiro .... Contralto
Federico Baciucco .... Tenor
Mayor and other local inhabitants

Note:. In the interest of uniformity, the parts of all characters are given in English throughout. An asterisk * indicates those portions of the text which have been translated from the Italian of the original libretto.

HENRY − INTRODUCTION

Notte e giorno faticar per chi nulla sa gradir . . . Night and day I have to work, for a most ungrateful jerk . . .

Or berk? No, make it jerk. Not that Don Giovanni was either. He was a right cunt, really, which makes it closer to berk. Berkshire hunt: cunt, says the *Ox Dic*, though if the derivation is correct then where does the vowel change come from? Why isn't it pronounced bark? Surely no one says Burkshire, do they, no matter what their extraction? Or do they? People say Mary Le Bone and Green Witch and Dull Witch − if you ask anyone in the tube for the proper places they take you for a foreigner. Which in a way I suppose I am. All these years on Italian soil have turned me into a nulliglot, a nulliglot nullity, so out of touch with the way English is currently spoken I oughtn't really be using the language for work purposes at all − only I have no other. My son Peter, calling from London, dismissed some- one to me the other day as a nerd. What is a nerd? Nurd? Nird? I didn't like to ask for fear of seeming one myself.

Italian scrappier still. Thank God I don't have to tackle the arias − only the spoken bits and recitative. Stay with jerk, then. It's going to be a pig's breakfast anyway, so who cares?

My reputation, Gaia wails. What reputation, for Christ's sake? A translation of Machiavelli's *Prince* with ten pages of wishy-washy commentary? A few articles here and there in the stuffier weeklies that'll survive only if someone somewhere happens to use the pages they are written on as wrapping paper for an object more valuable? A book on Vico that took me twelve years to write and that nobody save for a few old university fuddies has ever bothered to read? Can't even find my own copy now; think someone must have stuck it under one of the guest beds to stop the wobbling. An unfinished, unfinishable novel that even Gaia in her most geisha-like moments no longer cares to mention? Frig your reputation, you sorry old has-been, or might-have-been or should-have-been-but-never-was, and get on with the job in hand.

Non sperar, se non m'uccidi, ch'io ti lasci fuggir mai. How about that one? Fifteen beats: one two *three*, one two three *four* five, one two three four five six *seven*. Do not think, unless you kill me, I will ever let you go. Lamentable, could hardly be worse. Ugly wretch, unless you kill me, I will never let you go. Surprise: that one *is* worse. Woe is me, unless you kill me . . . Slightly better. Probably better still if I turned the phrase completely inside out like a sock, but the trouble is with translating, once you've made your first mould it's almost impossible to break free of it – you get cast in it like a sheep in a ditch.

Nobody will hear much anyway, nobody will notice. A one-night stand in an obscure Umbrian village – the words, foreign to most of the audience, wafting away into the hot oak-clad hills where the wild boar grub. Not pearls, no, just beads by the time I've finished with them – beads before swine.

And yet there's something beautifully fitting that my talents, such as they are, should be thus employed. It's the first graceful thing I've done in ages. Gaia blenches when she comes in with my coffee; in fact doesn't come in with coffee any more: doesn't think I deserve it. For seventeen years now she has kept the card house of my genius standing – fussing around it, preserving the balance, shielding it from all the draughts and tremors, shoving matchsticks under the base to keep it firm and righting any threatening list with a perfectly delivered little tap, unnoticeable to any but myself – and now, plapperty plap, and down it all comes. Her Henry, her revered Enrico, has laid aside all pretence of serious work and is devoting his summer to this . . . this *idiozia*, there is no other word for it. It's not as if it served any purpose; it's not as if anyone could act, or sing, or do anything except function as a target for obscenities from the local wits. O, *porco, porchissimo mondo*, it made her so angry every time she thought about it. Bringing Mozart to the villagers? Wake up, Enrichetto. There weren't any villagers any more: only a bunch of industrial farmers, probably far richer than ourselves, who kept their old houses on as convenient parking places for chickens and tractors and ageing parents – anything that cluttered up their fancy new concrete mansions. And, admitted that there were any, they didn't want Mozart either, they wanted Sting and Eros Ramazzotti. The whole thing was so dated and pathetic and embarrassing she wanted to curl up her toes and die.

I think the last two verbs go to form a pleonasm, but I never correct Gaia's English. It's the one thing about her that still reminds me how enchanting I once found her and (to anyone less jaundiced than my wretched self) how enchanting she presumably still is. She on the other hand corrects my Italian continuously – her optimism *re* my powers of improvement, in this and other spheres, simply refusing to die.

Gaia cara, Gaia bella, Gaia adorabile but not by me any more *adorata* – when did the end begin, when did the magical beginning end? How is it I can look on your beautiful bronzed body stretched out naked by the swimming pool and feel only a vague sense of amazement at the attention I once spent on it? How is it I can listen to your sweet husky voice, saying always kind and pleasing things – amusing, too, cheering, cajoling, flattering things – and feel only a traitorous craving for silence?

Oh, my sweet, I am so sorry, so ashamed at the way I'm made. How dare I feel surfeited on this meagre allowance life holds out to us? It is as if I were to see a butterfly with its one-summer-day span tapping its feelers and groaning at the monotony of its existence. Stupid insect, I would want to tell it, make haste, get going, lose not a nanosecond. To which no doubt it would reply, as I do, Oh, yeah? Then you get going, buster. I've seen it all till it's coming out of my antennae. There was a cure, I seem to remember from my childhood, for chicken-killing terriers, which consisted in hanging the corpse of its latest victim round the animal's neck so that proximity bred indifference and finally disgust. And that, my precious jewel, is what I have done with you by dragging you into this long and airless marriage. I have tied you tight until you rotted. Forgive me, oh, forgive me. Me and my fickle heart.

I even run the risk of getting fed up with this opera project before I've started. The translation, then the thinking up who's to play who, then the telephone calls with the dreary enthusiasms of those I've included and the huffs of

4

those I've left out. And then the readings and the rehearsals, and setting up the stage and fixing the lighting and getting someone to do the costumes . . . Oh, shit, I can't think what got into me. Were it not I already had the Mayor sold on the idea and skipping around like a small-town Diaghilev, I think I'd scrap the whole thing and go back to my stagnant novel.

640 in Italy, 231 in Germany, in France 100 and in Turkey 91 – that's one accusation at least you can't bring against the Don: he didn't tire easily, didn't give up the pleasure quest without a fight. (And thank the stars this is a sung bit, by the way: just imagine trying to put those numbers into English and still preserve the rhythm. In Bològna, 640 – I suppose one would have to get around it like that, by cheating.)

No, the further you go into the piece, the more you appreciate Don Giovanni's peculiar brand of virtue. OK he changes around a good bit but, as he says himself at some point, he's faithful to women really. *Au fond*, which is the area that strikes his fancy. In a collective rather than individual fashion perhaps, but he goes on loving them. If it didn't cross with his other plans I think he'd have another go at Elvira too – it's just that her timing isn't very good. If she got him at the right moment I don't think he'd say no to her, denial isn't part of his ethos.

And speaking of Elvira, I'll have another problem on my hands here. Gaia will want . . . has already sort of said . . . But I can't give it to Gaia, she just hasn't got the stature. Height neither, but it's not so much that, it's the tragic stature that's lacking. I do a lot to foster it of course – but for all my crotchetiness and meanness and the hundred little cruelties I inflict on her she remains basically intact: a strong, undentable little rubber doll.

Parents are like that too, or were till the old boy copped it: she comes of good *gutta-percha* stock. Gossip has it that old Mum Marchesa keeps a slave in her house – a keepsake from their diplomatic past in Eritrea or wherever it was – and I honestly wouldn't put it past her. I tremble when she comes to stay. Were it not for this small rag of title that protects me – thank the Lord very aptly in this case – and the fact that I am what she calls with rare restraint '*benestante*', her scorn would pour over me like boiling oil.

But back to Elvira. Who can I have to play her? That pill of an American woman – what's her name – Isobel Marchetti or Marconi or whatever it is, will do fine for Donna Anna. Just perfect in fact: beautiful, elegant, emotional, aggrieved, and deadly as a tarantula. (And Mr Marchetti or Marconi, with his trim little Pigling Bland figure, can squire her as Ottavio. No matter if he can't act – doesn't need to – just strut around on his trotters.) Gaia, if I have to include her in the cast for diplomatic reasons, will make a tolerable Zerlina, only I must sell it to her right; she mustn't get the impression she's being passed over as Elvira in favour of . . .

Of. Of. Of. Adele Klein? *Don't* want another American. Madame Rossi d'Avola – Flossie Rossi? *Don't* want another pill. Our neighbour Claudia? Hubby Francesco's already got the plum of Don Giovanni – would look like favouritism. Who then? Can it be our region has such a dearth of beautiful women with a bit of *douce douleur* about them? Where have they all got to?

Ah, wait a moment. What about that painter woman who lives out Perugia way? The one we're always meeting

6

round the place – the one with the joke husband who looks as if he's stepped out of a tobacco ad. Joanna, that's right. Joanna Volpi. Had dinner with them once, I think, or maybe it was only drinks. What about her? Beautiful certainly. Oh, yes, reminds me of my first wife Lucy before she started on the cosmetic surgery. Good figure. Good carriage, fantastic hair. Bit horsey round the nostrils, bit freckly, bit wooden the way she moves, but Gaia could teach her to loosen up a titch – she'd like to do that: it'd make her feel protective instead of jealous – and the freckles won't show on stage.

Yup, the more I think of it the more I like the idea. Can't think why she didn't come to mind immediately, this Joanna bird. Probably because we've never hit it off very well, she and I, that's why. I think she thinks I don't take her seriously as an artist, and I think she thinks right, I don't. Six-foot-square canvases smeared with what looks like absent-mindedly applied manure – not my scene at all. But, no, provided I can get her to stow away her brushes for the duration and belt up about Munch, I think she'd make rather a good Elvira. Best anyway that the *environs* can furnish. Can't be too fussy. Take a leaf out of Don Giovanni's book. *Purchè porti la gonnella* . . . Just as long as she wears a skirt . . .

Only I think she's mostly in army-surplus combat trousers, but *fa niente*.

JOANNA – INTRODUCTION

Notte e giorno faticar . . . At this point, when Leporello starts up his bolshie whinge against employers, I can turn the ruddy thing off. Or at least down a bit. The overture, no, the overture holds me mesmerised as always. Painful though it is I have to sit there supine – if you can sit supine: Bernard Woolley wouldn't allow Hacker to get away with that one – and let it wash over me in all its force, all its splendour. I wonder what Mozart felt when he wrote it? Did he know how good it was? Bet he did. Did he realise he had added a huge and beautiful jewel to the world's dowry? Made us all richer – the born and the as yet unborn? The function of the artist: to wrest some sense out of the welter of life and to transmit it to others to make them feel less lost, less lonely, less tossed around by Fate. Was he aware just how well he had succeeded in this task? The opera was performed for the first time in Prague in 1787, so the blurb on the disc tells me – did he ever think that more than two hundred years later a woman like myself would be sitting listening to those sounds that had come out of his brain and blessing him for them? Cursing as well, of course, but only because they ring so true and dig so deep.

Again, bet he did. I am an artist too, but a mediocre one. Like a small pudding basin I can turn out only so much, and feed only so many. This I know very clearly or I wouldn't be a mediocre artist, or even a bad one, I would be no artist at all – just a vain autistic dauber. And I think the same rule holds good across the board: talent, whether microbe size or genius size, needs carefully assessing before it can be deployed. If you don't know you've got it, or what you can do with it and what you can't, then you can't use it at all.

So I think you knew all right, Mozy, and you too, da Ponte: one day, many days, in many times and in many places, men and women, young and old, would listen, catch your message and be stirred by it, pierced through by it, buoyed up by it, whichever, and smile or laugh or cry according to their mood. No surprise therefore (apart from the technical aspect) to find in the month of June 1999, in a remote Umbrian hillside village, a forty-four-year-old Englishwoman sitting by a CD player, listening to a recording of the opera made thirty years earlier and crying her stupid eyes out.

I almost feel that dismal Henry Thirsk must have done it on purpose. He has the reputation of being a bit of a sadist. Ringing me up like that and asking would I play Elvira. Elvira, if you please: daft, pluri-betrayed, lovesick Elvira, always ready at the drop of a hat to forget, forgive and start all over again. Bet he was sniggering inside when he said it. Bet he's heard the gossip about Orso's latest and thought how neat the parallel would be.

But I'm not forgiving this time around and I'm not playing that silly moon-eyed cow for everyone to laugh at behind their pumpkin-seed packets. Sounds a pathetic idea anyway: recitative bits in English, spoken not sung, and all the arias and duets and trios and whatnots in Italian in playback. Disjointed. Ludicrous. Ghastly. What do the actors do when the music's on? Stand there and open their mouths like fishes? And what does the Italian sector of the public do while the actors are jabbering on in a language they don't understand? Jeer and throw tomatoes, that's what. Or talk. Or get up and leave.

No, I don't want any part in it. And particularly I don't want *that* part. The whole idea of amateur dramatics has always made me want to stretch out for the sick basin. Rich, idle, bored people thinking up ways to spend their money, pass their time and shift some of their boredom on to others in the process. Typical it should have come from Henry Thirsk; that's him in a nutshell: rich, bored and idle. A leftover from another age. They should put him in a tank of formaldehyde somewhere and stick a label on: English Milord; late specimen; species now extinct; *Deo gratias.*

The wife might mind, but only if she noticed, and quite honestly I think the chances are she wouldn't: he looks half pickled already, and the few times I've met him I don't think I've ever heard him utter a sound that wasn't tainted by a yawn. 'Wauuughh. Gaaaiah. Let's be going, sweetieh.' She's an aristocrat too of course, of sorts, or she wouldn't be able to stick it. All that languor. A mind shuffling about in velvet monogrammed slippers. A screen of flippancy put in front of everything he says so you can never nail him to anything, never tell what his real opinions are. Politics, morals, aesthetics – all just hired vehicles for his wit to cruise around in and then hop out of again if anyone taxes him. Is that yours? Do you really believe that? Are you ready to defend it? I've got a feeling he wrote quite a creditable book once upon a time, although I haven't a clue what about. But if he did, I imagine that too was done in a suitably detached fashion: 'One is tempted to think,' 'It would appear to be the case,' 'One could tentatively put forward the hypothesis . . .'

One could just tell him to get stuffed. Accidie, that's what he suffers from. Acid stomach too, no doubt. Packed full of acid like a battery. Or am I being unfair and is it me who's gone sour in this corrosive summer heat?

It's weird, I actually don't want him to come here. Orso, I mean. I really and truly don't. It's the first time in my life – in our married life – that I don't want to see him, or be with him, or even hear his voice on the other end of the telephone. I often used to say it – in the days when I knew that there was something up but that that something was nothing – but I've never before meant it. Now I mean it but I don't say it. Just go on gardening when I hear the ringing and pray that it will stop. When I'm in the studio I go one step further and leave the receiver off the hook. It worries me slightly on account of Vicky – her being so far away and everything – but anyway she knows she can always reach me through Amabile for anything urgent.

I can't be with him in his present state, it's just too painful. That mobile phone of his, oh, how I have come to hate it. I despise myself for deigning to notice, but I'm always on the lookout to see if I can see it stashed away in his clothing somewhere. Especially when he's in the garden: signals are difficult to pick up in this hilly region and more than once I've caught him prowling around near the tennis court, where reception is presumably better, doing a kind of Maori dance, up and down, up and down, with the wretched thing clapped to his ear. And if – as he rarely does – he leaves it lying around the house somewhere it's all I can do to prevent myself peering into the dial to check if there's a message. I'm hopeless as a rule with gadgets, but need has made me wily and I even know now how to get in touch with the answer service: what button to press, what number to dial, everything. That I haven't done so yet is only on account of the nausea: I see that little green light – *would* be green, wouldn't it? – and a wave of sickness comes over me, turning my fingers to jelly. (I did as a matter of fact eavesdrop on a conversation of his to one of his girlfriends once, mainly by mistake. I picked up the phone in the living room and he was on the line in the bedroom, talking to someone in such a tender voice I thought it could only be Vicky. *Amore. Piccolina mia.* Wrap up well against the cold in this weather, won't you, you are so skinny. Promise me you will? Promise? So like a fool I went on listening, smiling to myself and thinking what a good relationship they had, the two of them, father and daughter, especially when I wasn't around, until the truth suddenly dawned, and when it did the pain was so intense and overwhelming it winded me. Knowing is one thing: having the knowledge brought home to you through your senses is another.)

I think that was when I knew, almost in the second sense, through my guts, my winded diaphragm or whatever, that one day I must leave him. And now the day has arrived. It is over now, it is over. He must keep away from me this time, he must, he must. And stay away. The woman that's in me would no doubt survive another amputation – the waiting list, the anaesthetic, the operation itself and then the convalescence and the gradual return to a diminished state of something like health – but the artist wouldn't. It'd be my painting hand this time, the limb to go. I paint with a proud part of me and it won't bend any more without snapping and that is that.

Nor will it allow me to caper round a stage, playing myself, to gratify the whim of a foppish old dilettante nobleman who's got nothing else better to do. *Basta*. I will ring him and tell him so tonight when I reconnect the telephone. Or perhaps I won't even bother, just let the matter drop, plonk, into the waste basket where it belongs.

And now for God's sake let me go back to my canvas which, thin as it is, is the only thing at the present moment between me and utter desolation.

GAIA – INTERMEZZO
WITH FAX MACHINE

Il Castello – Montaldo – Todi
June 9th '99

Dearest Emily,
Simply to confirm that Henry and I are looking forward to seeing you and Wolfgang on Friday 18th of this month. Our usual driver unfortunately went and got himself decapitated during the winter – a rare and privileged death, says Henry, in this century – so we are sending a new one. His name is Federico. He looks very like the other, is in fact a cousin, but to be safe he will be wearing Henry's old straw hat that you say you would recognise even on the Day of Judgement, and will carry a carton with your name on. No fear, I will do the spelling myself this time!

What you so amusingly call human clothes quite unnecessary – our summer life gets every year more simple. Just one long dress maybe, as Henry has got himself co-involved in a dramatic production for our local *festa* – he couldn't say no, poor love, everyone was so keen he should do it and no one else – and I think he has you in mind as one of his *prime donne*. (Or should I say primadonnas in English, all one word with an s?) He will explain more fully at your arrival. Don't be alarmed, it will be a kind of joke, you know, not a serious piece at all. In the meantime my very best love,

Gaia

P.S. Forgive such a short message, but Henry is keeping me so busy – as you can imagine! Today I have to start typing out the parts for him, like a perfect secretary.

*AMABILE – INTRODUCTION OVER AN IRONING BOARD

Tutto il giorno faticar . . . What a lot of work this summer.
Beppe and I used to say when we were young, we were
working so we could take it easy when we were coming up
retirement age, but we were totting up the bill without the
innkeeper. Who could have thought the Almighty would
take our Stefano away from us like that – only thirty-two,
and strong as an oak, and such a careful driver? I know it's
a sin, but sometimes I wonder if the Heavenly Father minds
what he's doing. Look at all those ugly faces you see on
television – those drug dealers, those Mafia bosses, that
man who's chasing all those poor refugees out of their
homeland, wherever it is. If he's got to take people before
their time is up why doesn't he take some of those? But no,
it had to be my good hard-working boy with his wife and
family still to care for and his bank loan for the house and
taxi still unpaid. 'Don't you worry, Mamma,' he used to
say. 'No scrimping for you in your old age. I'll have you
going to church in furs like a proper Signora. I've got broad
shoulders, I have, I'll carry the load.' And now, if it weren't
for me and Beppe, his children would hardly have food to
eat or a roof over their heads.

Lucia's not a bad girl, of course, she does what she can,
but she's young to be a widow and with Stefano she was
accustomed to an easy life – you can't really expect her to
turn into a breadwinner overnight. It's something that she

17

got herself that job in the video shop, even if it does keep her out a lot and leaves little time for minding the children. And there again, at her age and with what happened she needs a bit of spending money for herself, it wouldn't be right to ask her to put all her earnings into the family kitty.

Only it is a burden. Oh, God forgive me for thinking like that – children are a blessing not a burden. But sometimes, after I've got the animals fed and given Beppe his breakfast and packed his lunch and seen him off to work, and done the shopping and called my mother-in-law and the young-sters and set them up for the day, and then come over here and got the Signora tidied up – and my word that studio of hers does get in a mess sometimes, bedroom too, not so much the kitchen – sometimes, when I get back I'd like to sit down in a chair for a moment outside the front door in perfect silence and look at the roses and listen to the birds. Instead of which I usually hear their voices from the top of the road and they're nearly always quarrelling: the little one has problems, the teacher says, and not to cross him; he saw the accident, you see, he was there beside his father when the drill on the lorry in front broke loose and crashed through the windscreen, doing what it did; it was a miracle he was spared.

So it's either squabbling, or else the kitchen's knee deep in water because they've shampooed the rabbits, or there's flour everywhere because they've tried their hand at pizza-making or Lord knows what. Last week they collected the eggs – twenty all told – and fed them to the puppies who sicked up their souls, poor little devils, all over the place. There's no knowing what they'll get up to and you can't really trust the old lady to stop them. It's not that she's lacking a tongue, very much the opposite, it's just she's grown a bit deaf lately and doesn't seem to notice. Sometimes – although it's not nice to be so critical – I think she even puts it on a bit, the deafness: she seems to hear the things she wants to hear all right – television, radio, gossip, no problems there.

Till recently I used to be able to tell all this to the Signora, and it helped me, and on the days we'd had a good chat I'd come back and keep my temper, no matter what. But just now she's got other things on her mind and I don't like to bother her with my problems. She was so good with the funeral expenses and all, I shall never forget. Anyway, mustn't grumble, the pay's good and the work's light compared to home, and it's good to get out a bit – makes a change, stops me brooding. And talking about brooding, there's that old hen I've got to deal with when I get back. Funny, I never used to mind that side of things – seemed natural, it's food, isn't it? It's the way the world's arranged – but now I have to steel myself to get it done. I'd ask Beppe, only he's all in after his quarry work, and in his heart I think he feels the same way I do. It's changed us, this thing, made us grow old before our time. Old and soft, and tired . . . I can't explain it, tired on the *inside*: the work's nothing, it's those children's voices, they go through me like a knife.

*ORSO MARIA – SERENADE TO A MOBILE PHONE

Little one. Why don't you keep this thing switched on? What was the point of my buying it for you if you don't? I go mad when I get that voice telling me to leave a message. What message can I send you without my body to spell it out for me? I need you. I love you. I want you more than food or air. Ring me as soon as you've finished work, at the number I gave you. One ring first, remember, and then the call. If for any reason I can't answer I'll disconnect and then call you back. Tonight I may be late – last client comes at seven-thirty and this one I *must* see: comes all the way from Geneva – but the sky would have to fall to stop me coming, and even then I'd manage somehow.

HENRY — ARIA

My father, who said little memorable during his lifetime, gave me one useful rule of thumb: never to be rude by mistake. And generally I have abided by it.

It now would appear, however, according to Gaia who is well up in these things, that I have made a most dreadful blunder in inviting Mrs Volpi to play Elvira. The poor woman is allegedly crowned with larger and more ramified antlers than a moose. Ooops. And how do I wriggle my way out of that one?

By insisting, I think. Not by back-pedalling but by taking the dilemma by the horns. Ooops again. I will invite her over and put my case before her. Appeal to her vanity, her kindness, her sense of humour if she has one. It would be a great publicity coup in a way to have a real wronged wife up there on the stage, wailing on about her real philandering husband — very topical, just the thing for a group of catty old expatriates like ourselves. Not to mention the locals who guzzle scandal as greedily as if it were their black beloved truffles.

Women's tastes are strange though. I think I would gird my tights and run a mile from Mr Volpi myself. Or several miles to be on the safe side. The spivvy specs alone would be enough to set me scuttling, without the Porsche and the tan and the aftershave and all the rest of the accoutrements. Was Don Giovanni so transparent with his wiles? Of course he was — only got to see that tawdry spiel he drags out for

Zerlina – and therein doubtless lay his charm. *Femmine*, as our new driver bloke says with such operatic despair – should rope him in as Masetto; good idea, think I will; part's short, English shouldn't be a problem. *Femmine*.

Now let me see, where have we got to today? Ah, yes, a little further on, with Elvria bursting in on the conflab between Anna, Ottavio and Don Giovanni, determined to spill the beans and open everyone's eyes and save Zerlina from a fate which poor little Zerlina herself seems to regard as highly desirable – best thing life's offered her yet. *Non ti fidar, o misera, di quel ribaldo core.* 'Don't you believe a word of it, he's only after . . .' After what? The only appropriate two-syllabled word I can think of is crumpet, but there's a limit to what one can do with da Ponte's resilient libretto and I think crumpet overshoots it. He's only up to mischief? Weak, flabby and coy. He's only out to con you? Ugly, that truncated con. He only wants to shag you? Correct and explicit but same thing applies with a vengeance. Fuck? *Idem cum vindicta.* To lay you, then? American, but the audience will be full of Americans. Don't you believe a word of it, he only wants to lay you. Oh, stop fooling around, Henry, you dirty old dawdler. Ah, I know, Don't you believe a word of it, his heart is cruel and fickle.

Like mine. I distance myself from the seducer, side with the victim, and all the time my Judas heart denies, deceives, betrays. I think it is partly why I dreamed up this ridiculous time-wasting project in the first place: so as to have a reason for shutting myself away in my study and exacting solitude. The novel won't wash any more as an excuse and Gaia knows it. In her concern for my literary success she creeps in when I'm not there and counts the pages; she knows exactly where I've got to, namely into a bog; I don't think I could even delete a comma without her noticing.

My friend Machiavelli, how close I feel to him at times like this. *Venuta la sera . . .* That passage enchants me; I think I'll put aside the libretto for a sec and do a little construal of Nick instead. Won't take long. '*When evening comes I return home and go into my study; and on the threshold I shed these grubby everyday clothes and dress myself in state. And thus attired I enter the ancient court of ancient men, who welcome me with kindness, and where I can feast myself on that food I crave and that is so right for me and for which I was born. With them there is no need to feel ashamed: I can ask them the reasons for their actions and out of their goodness they answer, and for four whole hours I am freed from all boredom and worry – money troubles, fear of death, all gone as I lose myself entirely in their world . . .*'

No good, can't capture the grace of the original Tuscan. Thoughts are born as sounds really – all of them. And translation from one tongue to another is as vain an exercise as the description of a piece of music. Ta, ta, ta, tum, says Beethoven, now with that he means . . .

But no, that's bullshit. I fell in love with Machiavelli long before I could penetrate his Italian. How could I fail to? How could anyone in my plight? His hand, stretched out like that across the centuries – taking hold of mine, giving it a squeeze. *Ho, su con la vita, Enrico!* You too have spent the morning arguing with the local woodsman and frittered away the afternoon on cards and wine and listening to the empty gabble of your guests? No matter. Come with me, put your thinking robe on, and we'll go into the haven of the head where all is orderly and meaningful and quiet. You pine like me among my peasants for intellectual company? Pick up your books, open them, step inside and join the club. No time-wasters here – if you don't like the conversation, turn the page; nobody will take offence. Xenophon? Yes, he is an old windbag. Let him be, spend an hour with Plato instead, he's always good for a natter. Drop in on Pliny Pa and see what he's up to in his plush new villa. Stop off by Catullus and let him tell you about his love life; lend an ear to Sappho strewing her fragmented jewels among the olives. Company? Solace? Conversation? Here in this paper world is the finest that there is. Kneel down and kiss the earth in gratitude that you possess the key.

I do, Niccolò, I do, believe me, I am no ingrate. But you say it yourself – in the end it is only ink and paper, and there are times when . . . I don't know if I can even explain this to myself . . . I'm not a bona fide intellectual, you see, I think that's the trouble. Had I written something . . . No, not even, were I *capable* of writing something worthwhile, something that could stand on its own amongst these other ornaments, something that, no matter how small it was, had a little niche that it could rightfully occupy, then I think I would have earned my membership fee and I would linger happily in this club of yours – one of the boys – one of the girls. As it is I feel myself a gate-crasher, a sponger, a usurper, here on tolerance alone.

Oh, bullshit again, Henry. You're lazy, that's what, you never finish anything. Put those letters of Machiavelli back on the shelf, *and* the Pliny, *and* the Ovid, stop moaning and get back to Don Giovanni so you'll have something to show to the reluctant Mrs Volpi when she comes. If she comes: hasn't bothered to give me an answer yet, but imagine manners are not her forte. May have to lure her with a lunch date. Blast.

*ORSO MARIA AND ANSWERPHONE – DUET

– Thank you for calling. Please leave a message.

– Hello? Joanna? It's me, Orso. No, don't leave the room in disgust if you're there, I just wanted to know how you are. I'm fine. It's pretty hot here. A parcel's come for you, I think it's books. I'll send them on by courier, OK. I . . . Nothing, I'll try not to bother you by ringing again, only . . . Nothing. *Ciao. Ciao.*

JOANNA – ARIA

This evening is the first time this summer that I sit outside with someone on my mind other than Orso, and the first time that when I shut my eyes I see something other than nightmarish images of what he is doing and where and to whom. (I don't know who this new girl is, don't think I want to either, but I can't help conjuring up pictures of her. I imagine her fair and rather awkward-looking – leggy like a colt. Not pretty so much as inspiring tenderness. The sort of girl I would take to immediately myself if I met her out of context, and vice versa, seeing that some of the things she likes in Orso have probably come to him through me: we've shaped each other a lot over the years. Orso is not adventurous in taste: he has a basic genotype or phenotype or whichever it is and sticks to it always, faithful in his faithlessness, constant in his whims. Probably fuses them all – us all – if truth were known into a single entity the way my mother used to do with her dachshunds. Oh, God, belt up, Joanna. You said you were thinking of someone else for a change, well, go ahead and ruddy think.)

So. Pushed by Amabile, who shamed me the other morning by her concern for my solitude (should be me sorry for her and not vice versa), I accepted an invitation to lunch with the Thirsks.

I groaned out loud as I drove there – too much drink, too many guests, too much small talk, much too small, and a whole afternoon probably thrown away by the time I could make a getaway and clear my head of fumes – and was twice on the point of turning back and ringing up with some last-minute excuse, but luckily I didn't because I actually enjoyed myself.

He's not such a bad old stick at all, old Henry. I misjudged him. And there weren't any guests, not of the kind I feared, only a strangely gruff and podgy niece with an ice-hockey champion in tow of such beauty it made you blink. And Gaia's a perfect honey when you get to know her: so vivacious, so pretty – no wonder he treats her with such care, as if she were a porcelain figure or something: she must be the focal point of his entire existence. Just a wee bit professional perhaps in the way she finds time for everyone and remembers everyone's favourite drink and food fads and whatnots – just a touch of the air hostess. But, no, that's bitchy: I'm merely envious of that lovely figure of hers and the way she seems – unlike me – to have got her domestic set-up under such perfect control. Husband included. Shouldn't think Henry ever looks at another female, not in that way. Mind you, he's probably not all that sexy either: fine skin, not much body hair, always bound up in his books. I was rather touched when he took me to see his study; OK, I knew he had a purpose and that he was buttering me up so as to get me to take part in this pantomime thing of his – you can't really call it an opera. But all the same he was so courteous somehow, so – what's the word I'm looking for? – so ceremonial, so quaint. 'Forgive me a second. Must change. Can't take you in there in my bathing trunks.' Why not? Because books and bare bodies don't go together? Because art deserves respect? He should see me with my air brush in the hot weather. But anyway I found it sweet rather than pompous. I found *him* sweet rather than pompous. And the way his face lit up like that when he discovered I already knew the words of the entire libretto by heart – I don't think he was buttering up then, I think he was really and truly pleased.

No, I'm glad I went, and I'm glad in the end I allowed myself to be won over. It was so silly of me really: over the telephone – well, these Umbrian phones are pretty crappy but even so – I'd somehow got it into my head that he wanted me to play Elvira. In fact I'm sure that was what he said, but I'm so muddleheaded at present I probably got it wrong. The fact is – much more fun and no worries about cutting such a lousy figure – he wants me to do the scenery. And how could I say no to that, even if I've got this exhibition pending in October? In a rash moment I offered to do the costumes too – thought I could make more of a statement that way, do something more homogeneous, more arresting – but, perhaps luckily, he said no, that would be asking too much and anyway he had to spread things thin because people got so touchy when they were left out.

Considerate old badger too – who would have thought it? People around here are so scathing – the imported lot like ourselves, I mean, not the locals – but I think it's just envy. His house is far the nicest of anyone's, and his pool is bigger and his garden is more luscious and better laid out, and he's so much richer – in proportion, I mean, to the effort he puts into *getting* rich, which appears to be nil. They say he's blasé and snooty and doesn't mix (why should he mix? I think he's better *un*mixed: crustier, per- haps, but fresher, like cornflakes), and the Americans poke fun at his English accent and the Italians at his Italian, and that neurotic Isobel Marcucci says she thinks he jeopardises the entire image of the foreign community, whatever she means by that, but I bet no one, *but no one*, of those he asks refuses to take part in the show.

Orso would, of course. Wouldn't think twice. That's one of the reasons I've stayed with him so long: the fact that worldly considerations don't cut much ice with him. Even that car of his, which with most men would be a status symbol, with him is a genuine passion. He loves it, the way he does his floozies. (Who aren't floozies either, would that they were.) Oh, sod you, Orso. Why aren't you a kind, faithful, adoring husband like Henry, or else just a straight-forward out and out shit? Either way I could cope, but not with this mixture. 'The elements so mixed in him that Nature might stand up and say . . .' I remember that from A levels.

Addio, that is what I say. *Addio* and not *arrivederci*. I have forbidden him to come here and will stick by my veto. Thank God I've got the answerphone installed at last, like that I don't have to risk contact even at a distance. There was a message from him when I got home this evening, but I played it back with my earplugs in that I use for swimming, so that I heard only the voice, not the words.

Thank God for paint, thank God for my work, thank God for this little weevil of talent inside me, gnawing away, wanting attention, wanting to be exercised, wanting to be fed. And in a minor way thank God for Henry Thirsk and his plan. You can't work at a painting all day but scenery's different, you can mess around with that for hours. It'll chase me out of the studio too and into contact with other

34

people. Good. Splendid. *Grazie*, Enrico, or Enrichetto as his wife so prettily calls him. *Grazie*. In return I'll get to work and try to think up something really really powerful for your sets like I promised.

*AMABILE – ARIA

Seven months today. People say time heals, and I'm sure they're right or we'd have walking wounded all over the place, but I can't really believe them. They say it's better to think of other things too – not to fret, not to keep going to the cemetery – but I don't believe that either, not for me. The Signora gave me a gardenia plant. Don't take it to the grave, Amabile, she said, keep it for yourself, I know how you love flowers. Well I do, and it's a delicate thing and needs a lot of watering, so I kept it on the porch for a few days like she said; but it didn't seem right somehow sitting there opening its flowers just for me; I wanted him to have it.

Silly, because I'm not sure I believe in God any more, or Heaven or the resurrection and all the things old Don Antonio taught us in catechism class when we were kids. But there it is: I wanted Stefano to have it and I couldn't rest till I'd taken it down there for him.

When I told the Signora she laughed. Nearly had me laughing too. Anyone else and I might have taken offence but with her it's different. I never had a daughter, and she's not the right age either, only ten years younger than myself, but she's a bit like that for me: a daughter. She sees things straight sometimes, like children do; makes those funny, true remarks, like a child. I'm sorry the Avvocato gives her such a rough time. I don't think he knows what he's got there. He's a kind man, mind you, very nicely mannered and doesn't let her lack for anything and I shouldn't be saying this against him – what he does in Rome is his affair and nothing to do with me – but he's not made of quite the same stuff. If he was a bolt of material, is what I mean, he'd be more the everyday wool kind, and she'd be spun silk. That's how I see it anyway, and Beppe agrees.

Now Beppe's sister Paola, the one who qualified as a dental nurse and then went on and married the dentist, gets cross with me when I say things like that. For her we're all on the same level. Silk and wool is fanciful nonsense, and I shouldn't be going out doing people's houses in the first place. If you need the money, she says – and my word we do need the money, especially now – then why don't you go back to cleaning offices? Or why don't you apply for a shift in the pasta works? It's less demeaning.

What's demeaning about what I do here, I'd like to know? Very well, Vicky leaves her underpants lying around sometimes and I give them a wash, but I do the same for my lot. *And* they don't pay me either. I don't see anything demeaning in doing a bit of housework for a decent family. Rubs off on us, says my sister-in-law. They may be nice to you but you're always the servant and we're the servant's relatives. Lot of old-fashioned rubbish to me. It might have been like that once upon a time – in fact it was like that: Beppe's mother remembers 'going into service' as being nearly as bad for a girl's name as going into a prison or a brothel. But it's not service now, it's helping out. Never got married, those ones, she says, ended up old maids. Not such a bad fate either, seems to me. Only yourself to look after, and days off would be days off. You could go to the hairdresser. Last time I went to the hairdresser was my niece's confirmation, and even then I had to go out half-way through with the rollers in to see to the ram – he'd got into the grain shed and blown himself up on barley, greedy brute. Next time it'll be our boys' first communion – Stefano's boys' – and that won't be for a few years yet. Lucky Beppe isn't particular and likes me the way I am, but it would be nice sometimes just to sit on a comfortable chair and let someone else fuss around you doing all the work.

Giovanna – the Signora – does her own, she's clever that way. Offered to do mine, too, take out the grey bits, but I'm not sure I trust her with colours – some of those paintings are such a mix they look like pig swill. Still, it's nice for her to have a hobby now Vicky's older. She said something about her and her friends getting up a theatre show this year for Saint Bartholomew's day in Montaldo over Todi way, and that's nice too. I should envy her her leisure, I suppose – Paola would say it's a shocking thing, grown-up people dressing themselves up like children at carnival and then taking good money from us to go and see them act. Patronising, she'd say: who do they think they are, these foreigners, moving in here and then throwing their weight around and telling us how to run our own show? What's wrong with the karaoke contest they held last year in Montaldo? But I don't feel that way myself. The money goes towards a new changing room for the football pitch, and I trust the foreigners to spend it right more than I would some of ours. That Nello did the collection last time for the *festa* here: maybe a coincidence but all we got to eat was bread and garlic and he buzzed around afterwards on a smart new motorbike. Smashed it up later and serve him right. Drugs, I shouldn't wonder, they all seem to be on drugs nowadays, the young ones.

That fellow Lucia's taken up with – he's got a bit of a druggy look about him. Works in a disco-club too and we all know what goes on there. Hope she doesn't bring him with her when she comes to take the boys out over the weekend – I feel so responsible for them to Stefano. *If* she comes, that is. Last month she only came twice; rang up the other two times at the last moment to say she was busy. I don't know which is worse, seeing their faces when she fails to turn up or worrying about them when she does and takes them off I don't know where or in what company. Mario, the little one, came back last time with a nasty blue bruise on his neck. Said Mummy's 'friend' did it to him for a joke, teaching him wrestling, but I didn't like the way he said it somehow. Didn't like to probe too much either, as it seemed to fluster him. Couldn't tell Beppe or he'd fly off his handle at the very thought: some stranger laying his hand on our boys.

It's all a bit of a worry. Not the way I'd thought life would be at fifty plus at all. Should think back on the old times, I suppose, listen to my mother-in-law talking about the wartime, and how they made acorn bread and wore no overcoats and used to trudge fourteen kilometres to work and back, and be thankful for what I've got. Lord, she does go on about it sometimes. I know it all back to front – the blackshirts, the partisans, the Americans, the way they carted off old Fritz to the prison camp because he talked so thick the Allied interpreters took him for a German. That's how he got his name: real name's Angelo but they've called him Fritz ever since. But it doesn't really help. If

Stefano'd died in a war maybe I could have seen some purpose in it, some reason that wasn't just a stupid lout of a lorry driver forgetting to lash his drill. The Avvocato says we'll get money out of the insurance people in the end, and says he'll help us too, but if I was rich enough I'd just throw the money back in their faces. Money, for a son. As it is though, we'll take it and be grateful.

I'd better have a word with him about it when he comes – remind him just in case he's forgotten. But this summer it's hard to catch hold of him. Hasn't been here for weeks. Wonder if there's anything serious up this time? Hope not for the Signora's sake. Beppe's different, or so I like to think, but men round a certain age can get themselves into tangles; they don't seem to have their heads screwed on the way we women do. Look at my brother Bruno and that Romanian. Twenty-three and him coming up sixty . . . One thing's certain, if he sets up house with her I'm not doing his shirts for him any more or having him round for meals. Let him eat goulash or whatever it is. There's a limit to everything, and sometimes, especially laundry days like today, I think I've reached it.

GAIA – RECITATIVE WITH LAPTOP, AND ARIETTA

Miss Ethel Briscoe
Miramare
12 Fosters Rd – Bexhill-on-Sea – Sussex – Inghilterra
June 20th '99

Dear Brissie,
Such a long time I'm afraid since I received your sweet
letter asking for news, but life has been so busy for me,
as you can imagine.

Yes, Mammà is well, thank you. She misses Papà
dreadfully of course, but her friends in Venice have
been very kind and close, and she still has Aki with her
– you remember Aki? The green noodles with the hairs
in them, and Dr Pallavicini's face when Bubi shouted
out, But, Mammà, Aki is bald! Those days were so
amusing, no? She has her bridge parties too, and Bubi
is nearby in Verona so he can get over to see her quite
often.

For me it is more difficult, as you can imagine.
Henry is working so hard and needs me with him
all the time. Italian husbands are getting so good
nowadays at looking after themselves, with the
shortage of domestics etc., but if I left Henry
to get his own meals I think he would die of
hunger. He is *so* unpractical it is just not true.

Not what I was taught to expect of an English-man at all.

You ask when his next book is to be published. Very soon we hope, but writers don't stamp a card like office workers and this summer he has set the novel aside so as to be free to work on the production of an opera. *Don Giovanni* by Mozart – not one of your favourites, Brissie, if I remember well; you used greatly to prefer Händel. (Who *was* German, you know, I'm not teasing, he really was.) It is a charity project for the aid of the children in the village here, so he couldn't really say no, and the organisers begged him so hard. They think he is the ideal person and, sad although it is to see him interrupting his real work for something so shallow, I must say I agree with them.

Misa is getting on better now in California. The start was difficult. She said to begin with she doubted you'd even taught us English because everyone around was speaking a different language! It is sad to have her so far away, particularly for Mammà, but all being well she will be coming over for Christmas, bringing the baby with her who none of us have ever seen. If she flies via London the way she did last time perhaps we could all meet up there? Wouldn't that be nice? What would you like me to bring you if we do? You used to have Marmite and suet sent out to you here – there must be something typically Italian that you miss? Or not? Only the weather, Gaia, I can hear you say. Only the weather. Well, it is wonderful at present but I'm afraid it is what you would call a tall order and I will

44

probably choose Baci Perugina in the end. And talking of *baci*, love and kisses from your fond ex-pupil,

Gaia

Voilà. Finito. Done it. Poor old Brissie. But it's funny, the unhappier I am the more I take refuge in the past. What is it? Lack of confidence? I'm afraid so: lack of confidence.

Oh, Lady Henry, what a way to talk. You have a position, a title, two beautiful houses, a husband who gives you anything you ask for. You are surrounded by friends, you are only thirty-five, which is no great age, and your skin is holding out well considering the way you sun it – why should you lack for confidence?

Why? Because I have let slip the handle of the knife, that is why, and now find it pointed against myself by the blade. When I married Henry he loved me more than I loved him – and that was right and as it should be, and the way it had always been with all the men in my life so far. I was the loved one, I was strong, I was safe. Now something unforeseen has happened: my love has grown while his has dwindled and I have become the weaker partner. I feel like I did in dancing school when we had to change sides: I hesitate, stumble, I don't know the steps. Before, everything I did, even silly things like running the car into a tree or ordering twenty cockerels from the poultry dealers so that each hen could have a mate, had a kind of poise attached to it. That poise has gone. I blunder through life now, and the more I blunder the more I know Henry resents me for it.

What can I do? Nothing. Keep quiet, move as little as possible, go on as before, pretend I haven't noticed. How

lucky, Mammà said at the wedding, there is such a difference in your ages. Eighteen to his forty – you will never have
to go through what I did with Papà. But numbers don't
come into it. Nor is it a question of sex – I think I'd
understand it better if it was. It's just that I have lost my
footing with him, lost my way, lost my touch. Sometimes I
think he actually hates me. But no, that is not possible, I'm
not a hateful person, I'm a lovable person. Everyone says
so, even the staff.

What worries me now is this opera business because it
brings everything out in the open. First he didn't want me in
it at all, and that was hurtful to begin with. But then I got
used to the idea: I could pass it off as a quirk, make a joke of
it, tell people with a little laugh, Enrico is like Einstein, he
likes keeping his wife in the background. Now it seems he
does want me, but instead of being pleased I am nervous. If
I'm awkward in my own home, just think what I'll be like
on stage. I'll forget my lines or make the wrong movements
or something, and Henry will be deadly polite, the way he
was at lunch the other day, and everyone – *everyone*, not
just our guests, which was bad enough – will see and notice
and be sorry for me.

That's what comes, I suppose, of marrying a man so
much cleverer than yourself. But is he, I sometimes wonder?
Is he really? Or is he just that *little* much cleverer that
prevents me understanding him? To a beetle mice must look
huge: is Henry only a mouse? I don't think I shall ever
know. In a way I hope I never shall. Oh why do things
always change? I'd like to feel young and pretty again and
in tune with all the world. Or else older and interesting like
Joanna Volpi, who looks as if she doesn't care if she's in

tune or not – let the others adapt. What I don't want to be is what I am now.

Spoilt bitch, go and try and be nice to your husband's niece and the Bung, as she calls him. (Wonder why? I asked Henry but he doesn't know either. Perhaps it's his surname. If he's the baby's father, we really ought to know by now what his surname is, but when I said this to Henry he told me not to be so typically bourgeois and Italian. How can I help it, though, if that's what I am?)

HENRY − ARIA

Io son per mia disgrazia uom' di buon cuore. I am, alack,
alas, a man of feeling. And so I am, blast it and shit by the
shovelful. What on earth got into me the other afternoon?
There I was, with my prospective Elvira all wined and
charmed and ready to grant my every request, and what did
I go and do? Funk it, that's what. Ask her to paint the
scenery instead.

Can you imagine anything more feeble? Putting a live
person who is nothing to me before Mozart who is everything. Or nearly – leave a space for Schubert. I am disgusted
by my softness. But there you are – one look into those
gold-flecked eyes of hers and I just couldn't go through with
it. Put her up on the stage like that to rant about marital
infidelity with everyone whispering, Who's that? The wife
of the lawyer from Rome – you know, the one who . . .
Haw, haw, haw. No, I just couldn't do it and that was that.

I will pay for my spinelessness, however, and pay double.
Not only will I have to put Gaia in the role now – she being
the only beauty left (and I must have a beauty, to stand up
to the Marchetti woman who plays Anna, otherwise it all
goes lopsided. My hopes in Emily were crushed when I saw
the tum: I'd no idea she'd expand so fast). Not only, then,
will I have to settle for Gaia and shift my gravid niece to the
part of Zerlina, but I will also have to endure Joanna
Volpi's dastardly attempts at scenery. She's all fired up
about it. Shite. The other way round would have been

perfect but there you are, too bad. Last winter Gaia even went and did a course in painting imitation marble – cost a packet it did too – and she could have marbled me a nice sober classical backdrop with pillars and things. Kept her busy and happy and limited the damage no end. Graveyard would have been a cinch for her. Now we shall have bleeding rashers of Bacon to contend with, no doubt, or strident echoes of the Weimar Republic in acid green and mustard. Powerful was the word Joanna used – dreadful word and dreadful prospect.

How is it an otherwise rather discerning female has this terrible blind spot with regard to visual aesthetics? And how is it I've put my backdrops into her perilous paint-stained hands? We talked for a while about the opera and it was strange, it was like talking to a twin, or closer still a *Doppelgänger* – someone who had made their way through the work by exactly the same paths and stopped at exactly the same places and been struck by exactly the same vistas. Unnerving almost. Unsettling certainly: after she'd gone I couldn't plunge myself into paperwork any more, or even paper-play; I felt as if her nearness had grazed me, leaving a raw patch that only she, paradoxically, could soothe.

Bad. Bad. But nothing to get worked up about. A, it could have been chance: approach her on literature and you'll probably find her idols are of the marketplace variety, meaning the airport bookstand. B, she can't be that discerning about people either or she would never have pledged herself to Mr Volpi. Who is, I repeat, a joke and a flat one at that. Orso Maria Volpi – how *can* you be called Orso Maria Volpi? In Italian it sounds like some Fascist hierarch. (Or so my leading man Francesco tells me, and he should know.) And in English it's dinkier than Beatrix Potter. Bear Mary. God Almighty. Bear Mary Fox.

Anyway the Foxes, dog and vixen, in their different ways have taken up enough of my time. Today I want to get cracking with the dance scene. Dripping with sex, it is, charged with rampant erotic energy. Which causes something of a problem inasmuch as my drive in that direction has dwindled to slug force or thereabouts. Does Gaia notice? Of course she does. Does she mind? Of course she does. Does she remark on it? Of course she doesn't, she is far too adroit: a diplomat's daughter with a wily old courtesan of a mother who probably taught her to fake orgasm in the cradle. It is she now who forestalls me with Not-tonight-Napoleon tactics, taking all my shame, all my reluctance on to her own two shapely, altruistic shoulders. *Scusami*, Enrico, I am so tired, I have done so much letter-writing/gardening/sunbathing or whatever it is she does. Conjugal rights are known as conjugal duties in Italian: I have come to accept the justice of the term. I cower, and then lecture myself and rally, and approach my task with the weariness of a professional Sherpa attempting his thousandth climb. (Burdened, what is more, by the unworthy suspicion that Gaia, consciously or not, is secretly shelving precautions in an attempt to conceive.) Fortunately at some point my mind, which is the trouble spot, switches itself off and friction takes over. But the sense of – what shall I call it? Sometimes it is so acute it feels like self-loathing, comes back even stronger the moment I am through. Life shouldn't be like that. I shouldn't be like that. Above all, pleasure shouldn't be like that.

Mozart and da Ponte have caught it beautifully, trust

them – the hedonistic paradox, the mischievous knot in which the grinning gods have got us tied. *Vogliam stare allegramente*, Don Giovanni bellows out in the ballroom scene. We want to be happy, we want to laugh, we want to experience joy. The opera is full of joyful passages, scattered through the score like stardust particles where you least expect them, but here, where the intent is explicit, you can hear desperation in the singer's voice and Death himself cranking up the mechanism of the roundabout. What we have we cannot want; what we want we *can* have – oh, yes, indeed, the hitch is not so blatant – but not on the terms on which we want it.

Why aren't I simpler made? Why am I so critical, so ill at ease inside my own head? Can't even look at that sentence without wanting to change it to Why am I not made more simply? which is fussy and old-fashioned, and a good deal clumsier as well. Why did the black fairy come to my christening, poisoning with a wave of her wand all the other gifts. You will be rich, Henry, you will have a good brain, a healthy son, two beautiful and complaisant wives, an easy life; you will be born in a period without world wars (touch wood: things look a bit dicey at present); famine and pestilence will not darken your doors, the worst thing you will suffer from is sciatica with a touch of the piles now and then, but wait – see this little seed here, this little grain of yearning? I will plant it in your heart so that nothing you have, nothing you do will ever satisfy you entirely. You will be fed honey and it will taste sour to you, you will lie on feathers and they will feel like stones. You will talk sense – compared to many others – and it will sound like nonsense to you; you will write, and you will be praised for it, and all the while you will know in this bitter inner chamber of your self that it is trash, trash, trash.

In short, poor Henry, you will never be an artist. The artist's soul at some point must break free of the censor – fly, soar, kick the dust off its heels and what the hell. This yours will never be able to do. Pregnant with possibilities you will lie there, earthbound, like a great swollen chrysalis (or is it pupa? See, you are already reaching for the dictionary. Can't make a mistake, eh? Can't risk looking foolish when you confront yourself in the mirror?) but your casing will never break, your wings will never unfurl.

Tough luck, Enrico. You are not the only one. Look at Nietzsche, look at Wittgenstein. What were they if not thwarted butterflies, grounded by too much brain? Look at Bacon – your Bacon, not Mrs Volpi's – look at your old friend Plato himself; think if he'd let rip and written plays as well as dialogues, and love songs to his catamites; think what other masterpieces he might have produced.

Ah, yes, but they had brain on the grand scale, these guys. When a brain's that big, the goods come out willy-nilly. Too many openings, too many doors. It's only middle-sized brains like mine that the censor can cordon off successfully. Berlin can be walled up – half of it, for a while; Los Angeles would be a different matter.

No. Counter-order. Don't think, you ninny. Don't think at all. Thinking is your downfall; pick up your pen instead and blooming well write. Finish this pathetic ant-sized task you've set yourself – no, ants move something like three hundred times their own weight – this flea-sized . . . no, fleas are far too athletic, stick with slugs – this slug-sized task you've set yourself and go on to the next stage.

53

Twenty-fourth of August is your deadline. Other people are involved. You can't disappoint them the way you so regularly disappoint yourself. It's nothing, you object. No, it isn't nothing: piddling though it is, it is *something*. My Great Aunt Florence used to travel the world with a maid who was seasick, and before every crossing, as a preemptive measure, she would shove a basin under the poor creature's chin and stand over her commanding, Do it, you fool! Do it now! I will follow Aunt Flo's example and berate myself until I retch.

* AMABILE – ARIA OVER A
BASKET OF CHICK PEAS

This is a sitting-down job. The old lady used to do it once, a few years back, but she says her finger-joints aren't up to it any more and I've no quarrel with that one (though I've got a sneaking feeling they might be if she tried). I must do something with my hands, even night-times when the television's on, and it's kind of restful to sit here in the half-light, fiddling, making the same movement time after time, trying to get it as neat and quick as possible, watching the pile grow.

The boys helped for a while, but luckily they soon tired of it as all they did was flick the peas round the room with their fingers to see who could shoot the furthest. I didn't like to stop them: young ones need a laugh. Now Fabio's dropped off, thank goodness, and Mario's going that way too – fighting against it of course: he's had such nightmares ever since it happened that he's scared of sleeping. And old grandma's watching the variety show like a hawk – all those bare bottoms don't seem to shock her in the slightest, she's modern that way, almost more than I am. And the dogs outside are quiet for the once, and Beppe's gone round to the bar to watch the card players – still doesn't like to play himself but it's a step in the right direction – and as for me, well . . . I can't say I feel at peace because I don't, but I feel resigned. Quieter inside. Not so angry somehow. I can tell myself he's dead without a scream welling up; tell myself I'm never going to see him again and accept it as the truth. Couldn't do that before.

Giovanna – she keeps on wanting me to call her that and at last I'm getting round to it – Giovanna was more herself this morning too. It cheered me up just to see her. Lately the ashtrays have been full of stubs and you could see from the lay of things that she'd been up late, reading or pacing round the studio or whatever she does when she's there alone. But today everything was tidier – hardly any work for me, though in a house that big you can always find some – and after I'd done the kitchen and the bathroom she came up behind me with a rope in her hands – gave me quite a fright – and said she was going to tie me to a chair if I didn't stop. So I did, and we sat down on the terrace outside, underneath the vine, and had a nice long talk, best part of two hours.

I know what's up now. She confided in me, got it all off her chest. He's playing around again like I thought, only this time she says it's worse than the others and she's put her foot down, forbidden him the place. Quite right too. Should have done it years back, I told her. Men are like children that way: need a slap every time they put their fingers in the jam jar. You're a fine one to talk about slaps, she said, those grandchildren of yours can get away with murder. But anyway she knew what I meant.

Too forgiving, that's what she is, too ready to see everyone's point of view. Dirty scheming little hussy, that's my opinion of the girl: going round with a man old enough to be her father, filching money off him like as not, and all the time knowing he's got a wife and a home and a grown-up daughter – should be ashamed of herself. Disgusting.

No, it's not quite like that, Amabile, she says, it's not quite so simple. This girl's probably in love with him. I fell in love with him too – what wrong has she done except to commit the same mistake as I did? Poor child, she's Vicky's age, think if a thing like that happened to Vicky, what would you say then?

Easy. If it was Vicky I'd give her a piece of my mind. But Vicky's not one of these brassy young flitabouts, she's not involved with a married man, she's got her nice young boyfriend, Leonardo, from the university, and she sticks with him. Don't you mention her in the same breath as that other one, I told her. Vicky's my pet, I've seen her grow, she's like one of my boys to me.

That made her laugh for some reason: she didn't realise I was serious. You do me good, Amabile, she said. Go on, keep talking, tell me what you think I ought to do about Orso. Am I being too hard on him, refusing to see him like this? Shutting him out of his own house? It is his house, you know, he's still the one who pays the bills.

The Avvocato? Not a bit of it, I said. Shut him out and leave him out. I wanted to add something about our old ram and how we cool him down when he gets above himself that way, but it didn't sound respectful. An employer is an employer, and to me and Beppe the Avvocato has always been as good a one as you could ask for. In fact – only I wouldn't say this to Giovanna, she's soft enough on him already – I can see more or less what they see in him, these girls. Kindness, and nice looks for a man his age, and nice manners and always beautifully turned out, not to mention his position – it's enough to turn quite a lot of heads.

I'm sorry for him in a way, you know, she said. (I think she'd find pity for the devil if she came across him.) Men are so bad at coping with death. Haven't you noticed that with Beppe? How they run away from it, I mean?

I couldn't see the connection for a moment. She does say strange things, but it's no use getting resentful because there's no malice there at all. Then it struck me how Beppe goes all silent whenever I mention Stefano, and how he never comes to the cemetery, not even to collect me – lets me walk all that way in the heat, which isn't like him at all. Do you think that's what it is, I said? That they're weaker than we are that way?

That's what it is, she said. We women come to terms with old age first, long before it hits us, and then we tackle the problem of death. Head on, no cheating. Men, no: they shelve old age, shove it away from them, and then when death comes on the scene they have to face the two together and it's too much for them. Orso's running away from two unbeatable enemies, that's what he's doing.

Fancy way of putting it: to me he's still chasing after skirts, but there may be some truth in what she says. I've always thought of Beppe being the stronger of the pair of us, but if that's really so then why is it I can't talk to him about Lucia? There's something wrong there, I know there is: looks all peaky, hardly bothers about the boys at all now, just a quick call now and then – How are they getting on? Well, they're all right with you, Ami, I know I can rely on you, don't bother them if they're playing – and rings off again. And she's smashed the car up twice – nothing serious, just the bumpers, but it shows she's not got her mind on what she's doing. I spoke to her mother about it after mass last Sunday, but she's scattier than the daughter. Send the boys round to me, she said, all huffy, and loud so that everyone could hear; send them round to me if you're fed up with looking after your own son's children. Made it sound as if I was the one at fault. But it's got nothing to do with wanting to be rid of them – the house would be so empty without them now – it's more that, well, Lucia is their mother after all, and they miss her, and if she's in trouble . . .

You think she's on drugs, Giovanna said. Straight out like that, hardly a question. It's exactly what I do think, though I didn't know it till she'd said it. Drugs are a new scourge on us in this part of the world – the people you'd normally go to for help like Don Filippo and old Doctor Scarponi don't seem to have much in the way of remedies. Prayer's not going to get you far, aspirin neither.

Not that Giovanna had much advice to offer either really, but it was something just to be able to talk about it without feeling ashamed. Foreigners of course are better that way: less critical, more experience. I asked her if perhaps she'd have a word with Lucia herself but she said it was no use, that when they were on the stuff they lied like shamming footballers. Don't give her any extra money, was all she said. Don't cast her off, don't make her any unhappier than she already is, but don't on any account give her money.

Bit late I'm afraid because that's exactly what she was after last time she rang: money. She said it was for the lawyer in Perugia, the one that's handling the case for us, and stupid me I didn't think to check. Sent off a postal order next morning for half a million lire, which'll leave a hole. Didn't tell Beppe either because, like I said, he doesn't like me touching on the subject. Now I'll be in double trouble: out of pocket and in hot water with him. What I'd really like is to get her into one of these communities before it's too late – these places where they know how to deal with them. But there again Giovanna says it's no use pushing. You'll have to be patient, Amabile, she said, and wait until she does it off her own bat and in her own time.

Only the fact is, I've never had much patience: I suppose I'll have to learn it. There, that's that big pile finished. Only this little one left and then bedtime.

*ORSO MARIA – SERENADE TO A MOBILE PHONE

Little love, little star of mine, where are you? Don't be cross about last night. I couldn't help it, the case is so important. Look in the papers if you don't believe me, or don't you read them? What do you read, I wonder? Tonight I will bring you Leopardi, and we will turn the lights out and drag those filthy cushions of yours out on to the terrace and . . . Time nearly up, tell you later. A kiss on your eyelids. Can't wait, can't wait.

JOANNA – ARIA

I drew Amabile yesterday while we were talking. Sometimes I wish my profession were more practical. What can I do for her? Oh, I know, I can lend her money for a while to bridge over the gap so that Beppe doesn't notice, and I can give her clothes and stuff and have the boys round to swim, but these are things that come from the everyday side of me and that anyone could do. I would like to be able to give her something from me, painter. Better her life in some tangible way, soothe that ghastly wound she carries about inside and makes no fuss about, no fuss about at all.

She is the best person I have ever known. Not without faults, which would make her insipid, but with faults that are somehow qualities. Loves gossip, for example, but only because her character is so bubbly; loves running through the misfortunes of others, but not to gloat, merely to participate. Doesn't say particularly kind things or think particularly kind thoughts – too shrewd for that by far – but rolls up her sleeves and goes ahead and does kind actions: every time a coconut. Even this loss hasn't damaged her for other people: she's just as nice and easy to be with as she was before. I don't feel, for example, that I have to treat her in any special way on account of it – which contradicts what I've just said, but I don't. She bears no grudges, that's what's so wonderful about her; nothing is owing to her. Which I suppose is what makes you want to give.

Anyway I love her like a sister. Curse that miserable

Lucia for putting this extra burden on her shoulders. Poor girl, I shouldn't say that, she's got her own sorrows to drown, but surely she could have found some other less destructive way of drowning them. Drink would have been better; work would have been *far* better. And work works. Look at me. Blasphemy almost to put my trouble on a par with theirs, but this time the break's so final that it *is* bereavement of a kind. I shan't ever be with him again, not in that way; never again will we form a unity. Oh, I suppose I'll see him: I'll have to eventually, the division of certain things will be so infinitely tricky we can only do it ourselves. Books, compact discs, photographs. Pictures. God, the pictures! The ones I've painted of him and for him – are they his or are they mine? The ones we bought together, whose are they?

No, it will be such agony it doesn't bear thinking about. But in the midst of all this pending mayhem what am I doing? Working, that's what, and slowly slowly beginning to find myself – or lose myself or whichever it is – in my work. I've got three things going at the moment – four if you count the catalogue: the last canvas of the Elision series: E4, this almost academic or at any rate figurative portrait I've decided to do of Amabile, and Henry's scenery. Which is to be changed in the interval between the acts, making five different tasks altogether, five different embryos, all dependent on me to bring them into being.

Of the five it is funnily enough the two scenery projects that seem to clutch at me more urgently when I go into the studio. Yesterday I drove round to Montaldo with my pad, on which I'd done a couple of quick sketches just to give his languid Lordship a vague idea of the direction I'm taking and to check them against the space in the square as I remembered it, and he was so keen on what I'd done that I got caught up by his enthusiasm.

Perhaps intrigued is more the word than keen. He wanted to know why I wasn't going for traditional painted backdrops – I don't know why he thought I'd deliver him those, it'd be a crime to use a backdrop in that setting, like hanging a dirty sheet in front of a Van Gogh – and where I intended to get a juke-box, and whether all the low-strung wires wouldn't interfere with the actors' movements, especially in the dance scene, and what function a pile of miscellaneous objects made out of foam rubber would have, and why they needed to be metallic, and how they could be made to look so, and what pertinence any of this had to seventeenth-century Spain.

I tried to explain everything as best I could, but I'm not used to going into my reasons for the things I create and I'm afraid I was a bit incoherent. Some reasons I didn't even know till I'd said them aloud, and these were mostly rather intimate reasons that I would rather not have given. The tawdriness, for example, of the seduction scene; the fakery – I wanted to get this over to the audience, and that was where the objects came in. Fake objects, glittering but cheap, and made of foam rubber for the simple reason that Don Giovanni and Zerlina have got to lie on them. He in both senses, she in one, but anyway they've got to be fairly soft. Also I thought – I mean there's four different scenes altogether in the first act and you can't go changing things round too much in a shoestring production – I thought it very fitting that Don Giovanni's equivalent of a bachelor flat should be cluttered up with bric-à-brac – it gives an idea of his collector's spirit. At the same time, being brightish and catching the light well, the objects wouldn't look too out of place in the opening scene of the courtyard, nor would they clash too badly with the village street, and in the last scene, the ballroom, the actors could pick them up and dance with them and get them off the stage like that. Not that they're that wrong in a revel either: the gaiety has such a forced air about it, I've always thought. The wires? Well, the wires are meant to get in the way a bit: they suggest divisions between place and place. I've never done theatrical design in my life, but we did a bit of theory in art school and it was a trick I learnt there; coiled space, layers of reality, that sort of stuff.

Henry's a good listener. Perhaps too good. 'You put a lot of yourself into your work, don't you?' he said when I had finished. 'I never realised. From the paintings, I mean, it's a bit hard to deduce. I think it's very brave of you, you know.'

Caught me quite off balance. I wasn't expecting a personal thrust like that, I thought I'd been so good at camouflaging my stupid woes. But, no, of course, everyone knows, that's part of the misery of it. You're the one who's sinned against, and you're the one who bears the shame.

I quoted Elvira at him to turn it into a joke: the bit where she goes off her head and says she wants to blow Don Giovanni's cover and expose his wickedness to the whole wide world. *Le tue colpe ed il mio stato vogio a tutti palesar*. Dotty but they were the only words I could think of. 'She doesn't, though, does she?' he said, looking at me very closely and not taking up the joke angle at all. 'She forgives him. Right up to the end.'

66

I was getting a bit out of my depth. I don't know him at all well yet, and I'm not that sure I want to, and the situation seemed so un-English somehow – the two of us standing there in the middle of the square, under a burning sun, discussing – well, basically discussing my husband's adultery, but I really did feel a terrible urge, just for a second, to blurt everything like I did to Amabile the other morning. God, I must be going off my rocker, it's all this solitude.

Luckily I held firm. Just looked a bit embarrassed – which I was – and went on to ask him, in much too loud a voice, about the costumes and the lighting technician. Costumes don't matter much really, the camper the better, but with all this emphasis on metal, lights are going to be vital.

'You'd better speak to Masetto about the lighting,' he said, and gave me the telephone number of the guy who's playing this part and doubling as electrician – real name Federico. So, unlike the sets, this side of things obviously doesn't interest him at all. Which is funny. He's probably not technically minded. How old is he? Coming up sixty I should think. Not all that much older than Orso, not even all that much older than myself, but in some ways he seems to belong to another generation, almost another century. I could picture him very well doing his writing by candlelight and sprinkling sand over the finished page.

'And the costumes?' I had to remind him.

'Umm.' I had a sudden feeling he hadn't made any provisions about them yet, but perhaps I was wrong because the hesitation was only slight. 'The costumes. Yes, the costumes. The costumes are in the hands of

Florence Rossi d'Avola. Do you think you can get on with her all right? I mean, can the two of you liaise?'

'What if we can't?' I loathe Flossie Rossi. Shoulder pads and gypsy earrings and hair dyed the colour of Guinness. I hate the word liaise too.

My voice must have sounded rather snappy – solitude is bad for me that way, I lose my monitoring equipment – and I half expected his sadistic side to show itself in reaction but it didn't, quite the reverse. 'In that case,' he said, swallowing in a funny abrupt way as if downing a fly or something even larger, 'there's no contest: Florence goes overboard and you stay.'

Such meekness totally disarmed me, and instead of snatching my chance, as I suppose I should have done if I'd been a bit tougher and more energetic and quicker off the mark, I found myself agreeing to everything: liaison, Flossie with her Joan Collins styling, and probably shoulder pads in the costumes as well by the time she's through. Only stipulation: that she consign all her stuff to me before the night so that I can rip the wretched things out and do a bit of doctoring with scissors and paint and whatnot. Ya ha! Extraordinary, but I'm beginning almost to enjoy this business. Henry took me to have coffee in the little shop by the church before we left, and read me bits of his libretto and talked to me about the difficulties of translation in general, and although I didn't know quite what to say to him in return – his rendering to my mind is pretty wild – it was so nice sitting there with him in the sun, looking out into the piazza, with the swifts swooping down on us and all the old codgers playing cards and drinking wine and thumping their tricks down on the table – *Busso! Striscio!*

Asso mai ti lasso! – that I forgot Orso entirely and everything connected with him, and the tight feeling I've had in my innards ever since I've been here disappeared and the coffee slid down me smooth and unhindered like honey. I felt whole again, an independent person facing life with zest and curiosity and a tinge of pleasant fear, the way I did when I was a girl.

I never had an English lover. I wonder why? And I wonder why this thought should strike me now? And in this funny melancholy way, as if it entailed a loss of some kind, a deprivation? Even as a child at school, when we invented boyfriends for ourselves, mine were always foreign. Swarthy, macho, hairy as apes. The beach boy in Brittany, the Portuguese priest who stood in for Father Kelly when he went back to Ireland on holiday, the Spanish doctor who came to see me in his tennis clothes when I was down with the grippe in Majorca – these were the stuff my dreams were made of. Why should it have been so? Was it something to do with language? Did my own language frighten me or something? Did a native English speaker represent too much of a challenge, or threaten to come too close? Too late now to trace the cause, but whatever it was, as Henry was speaking – reciting some bit of poetry or other that I'd never heard before – I felt a great tug of attraction towards him that had nothing whatsoever to do with sex but more with recognition, homecoming.

I grinned at him over my coffee cup and he grinned back in exactly the same way and at exactly the same moment, and the thought came to me that by onlookers we might easily be taken for brother and sister.

Funny thing was too that I left my pad on the table by

mistake, and when I went back for it afterwards the man who'd served us coffee had come to just that conclusion. 'Oh, it's yours, is it, Signora?' he said, as he brought it out from behind the counter. 'Here you are then. I was keeping it for your brother, I thought it was his.' Might have been probing of course, in typical Umbrian way, to find out what connection there was between the two *forestieri* and if it looked like fertile ground for gossip; but I don't think so, I think it was his true opinion.

Never had a brother either and never been bugged by it, but one like Henry would really have been nice.

FLORENCE –
INTERMEZZO ON A POSTCARD

Harrods – Haberdashery Dept
Knightsbridge – LONDON S.W.1 – Inghilterra
July 2nd '99

Please send by express mail the following goods and
debit to my account:
Contessa F. Rossi d'Avola, Il Mulino, Fratta Todina,
PG. Italy:

50 yards broderie anglaise edging, the widest you have
    (white)
30 yards organza, the finest you have (oyster-
    coloured)
24 yards rose-pink velvet ribbon, 2 inches wide
12   "   dove-grey   "   "   "   "   "
12   "   moss-green "   "   "   "   "
16 prs. silk-covered foam-rubber shoulder pads
    (white)

Many thanks for your prompt attention,
Yrs faithfully,

F.R. d'Avola

*JOANNA – INTERMEZZO
ON A SCRAP OF PAPER

Amabile,

Gone to Perugia for brushes. Could you be an angel
and boil up this spinach for me – it's already washed.
Also could you ask Beppe when he goes down to S.
Giovanni in his van to pick up an order for me from
the ironmongers? Here's this list in case they leave
anything out:

2 × 50 m. rolls thin steel cable, thickness of
    maccheroni
2 × 25 m. rolls copper cable, slightly finer
12 rolls heavy tinfoil
50 m. flexible black tubing plus joints, diam. 15 cm.
5 kgs. foam rubber, width 20 cm.
10 kgs. plastic sheeting
6 sprays silver paint
24 large hooks, plus expansion screws and clamps

Thanks. They also said they'd put by some hemp sacks
for me if they found any in the warehouse, but these
are a gift from old Sig. Felice for the *festa*, and don't
need paying for.

J.

*GAIA – LAMENT ON A LAPTOP

Darling Misa,
Don't gawp at me writing to you like this, but over the
telephone it just isn't the same thing. I can never
remember what time it is with you either, and Henry
has told me so often that I daren't ask any more, and I
don't want to wake you in the middle of the night
when you get so little sleep with the baby and all, so
here I am writing. Like we did when I first went to
London, do you remember? When we were frightened
of Mammà listening in to our conversations? Which
she did, the naughty old thing – she was always
terrified of me getting pregnant and leaving it too late
to have an abortion, and now it's the opposite and
she's terrified of me remaining childless.

As I am just a bit myself. Oh, Misa, I do miss you.
And I do miss Venice and the carnival and the parties
and all the friends we had there. I got out all my
photographs yesterday and started sorting them: I'm
going to buy a big album and stick them all in.
Regressive behaviour Henry's niece said when she
found me at it, and she's probably right, but why
shouldn't I regress if I feel like it? And who is she to
criticise anyway.

Just between the two of us I find her rather difficult –
Emily. So coarse and offhand and scruffy it's difficult
to believe her background is what it is. The English

aristocracy is different that way, I notice – seems to have no pride any more, no rules about keeping up appearances, especially the young. *And* we've got her for the whole summer too. I think this is slightly unfair of Henry because when I asked if we could have Pussi and Tòto – as company for me, you know – he groaned and said, For Christ's sake no guests this year, he had enough on his plate as it was, and now his niece moves in on us for the entire season, second year running. Boyfriend, partner, baggage attendant or whatever he is, is being sent north to his own family, which is a pity because, although dreadfully shy and *ruspante*, at least he was nice to look at, whereas Emily . . . Oh dear, I am mean.

Misa, I'm in such a mess. I'm like a seesaw: I go through moments of thinking I'm too much in love with Henry to be able to go on living with him happily any more, and then I swing the opposite way and think I'm not in love with him enough.

Sometimes he makes me furious. I mean, there he is, so clever and talented – you remember the reviews I sent you when his book came out? How good they were and how one critic said he was like some famous German writer whose name I don't remember? Max Someone or other. Weber, I think – yes, Weber. Well, what's he up to this summer? I give you three guesses. Finishing his novel? Wrong. Giving it up and starting another one? Wrong. Doing endless research so as not to have to come to grips with writing at all? Wrong – that was last year. No, this year he is getting up an opera, if you can imagine it, for the village people. To raise money for a changing room for their dreary football pitch to replace the old one that collapsed in the earthquake. One night of lunacy which nobody except possibly the players will enjoy or appreciate or remember, and two and a half months of what may sound amusing in the idea stage but which when you get down to it is in fact just pointless slog and bustle. I've had to type out all the parts, for a start, which meant cutting my nails and spending the best part of the day indoors when I could have been sunbathing out by the pool. *Uffa!* Then I've had to make dozens of telephone calls to people I wouldn't normally have rung at all and listen to them chirping about the 'fun' and the 'excitement' and how young it makes them feel, bla bla, and have all sorts of odd-bods over for meals who I'd never normally have invited and listen to the same all over again. And then – worst of all – I've had to learn, or will very soon have to, before Henry starts wanting to rehearse us without copies, my own tiresome part. Which is so much longer and trickier than I'd expected, it just *won't* stay in my head. I was always hopeless at learning long things by heart anyway. Remember Brissie and *Hiawatha* and how she used to despair? Plus which it contains words like *cimento* and *numi* and *pietade* that I have to think twice about in Italian, let alone in Henry's translation. We had a read through the other evening and it was shaming. All the others, except for me and our poor driver man who's been roped in by Henry as a sop to the locals and is totally at sea, worse than I am, were rattling off their lines word perfect like goody-goodies at school, while he and I sat there rustling our librettos, desperately trying to find the right place. I was almost in tears by the end of it. I used to think I liked Mozart – the tuney bits anyway – but now the whole thing just makes me yawn and/or shiver.

The character I play is called Elvira, and she's an all-round loser, and I think it brings bad luck to play a role like that, especially at this particular moment of my life. Her sung part's very weepy and waily too, and Henry insists on my opening my mouth wide to fit the playback, which I hate as it's not at all becoming. How did Callas manage, I wonder, and still stay glamorous? Luckily the costumes are being done by this very talented friend of ours – married to Sergio d'Avola's brother, once an admirer of yours, no? – so at least I'll look nice from a distance. Sets on the other hand have been taken over by this rather intense, arty woman Henry's so keen on all of a sudden, and will probably be dreadful. What he sees in her work I just can't imagine. We were taken to see her studio once and it was so embarrassing – no one knew what to say: the paintings weren't paintings at all but patches of ploughed field stood upright. (And, no, Misa, he doesn't see *that* either. How can I be so sure? Well, because after so many years of living with him I know my Enrichetto inside out. He hates tall women, for one, especially if they're clumsy, and this one is a *carabiniere* with boots on. He hates bossy, talkative, assertive women, and this one holds forth, gabble, gabble, on every subject under the sun. Plus which, not to be snobbish, but she's not quite, quite from the same sort of circle as ours, if you see what I mean. Not a long way down the social pile like Emily's hillbilly – he would like that, that might be rather dangerous – but from somewhere in the middle section which, typical English, is his least favourite spot. If they went to a hotel together she'd probably ask where the Ladies' was, or could she have a dessert sent up afterwards or something, and it'd turn him off quicker than if she told him she had Aids.)

No, it's not this woman. (Who on the contrary I feel rather sorry for, as she has this desperately attractive husband who, unlike Henry, really does give her a lot of problems that way. Or so they say – wouldn't know myself – wouldn't mind finding out either!) It's me. It's Henry. It's something wrong between us that I can't put my finger on. I'm not comfortable with him any more because he's not comfortable with me. I know he thinks I'm stupid, and I probably am compared to him, but I'm not as stupid as he thinks. Nor as unfeeling. I wound easily. I worry. Sometimes at night, when he's gone off to sleep, I creep out of bed again and go downstairs and watch television, just to try and stop the flurry in my head. The other night I got Fellini's *Otto e Mezzo*, and that was worse, as the unhappy wife in it does just the same – stays awake and frets and smokes cigarettes. I lit one myself and stared at the screen and it was like looking in the mirror. (I think I might try doing my hair like Anouk Aimée in the film too. Do you think it would suit me?)

You were always the clever one, Misa, help me, tell me what's up with him, where I go wrong, what I can do. Ring me – it's probably better – whatever time is most convenient for you for a chat. Ring Collect, so that Astolfo can't complain. And say nothing to him about my troubles, nor to Mammà either, who would merely tell me to smile serenely and buy new underwear.

Fondest love, G.

HENRY — ARIA

Oh, Henery, Henery, what is happening to you? If anyone else had brought me those admirably designed plans for wrecking my production I would have torn them up in front of their pretentious noses. But Joanna's nose is sprayed with a mesmerising formation of freckles, a constellation, a cluster which spaces out towards the cheekbones in Fibonacci pattern, and instead of telling her what I really thought of her barbaric punk scrawls and what she could do with them I found myself feigning appreciation. Or the closest I could come to it.

Deeper and deeper water. As she enlarged on them I found myself listening too, and the curious thing was I almost began to see a point to them. Enough anyway to prevent me from being able to say that the whole idea stank.

What the heck, I thought to myself. On the one side you risk hurting the sensibilities of your audience, who probably aren't going to have any anyway, and on the other side you not only risk but are pretty well certain of hurting hers. Which do you opt for? No question. She'd obviously put such a lot of thought into the matter. And such a lot of herself too: those wires, those trashy baubles which I presume stand for her husband's conquests — it was like being granted a perch on the psychoanalyst's chair. In a properly organised world that swine of a Volpi wouldn't be allowed to come anywhere near her, let alone near enough to wound.

I would never have dared ask – it's none of my business – but she interpreted my admiration for her artistic courage as a comment on her private life (what else can you say to someone when they show you something hideous they've created? Brave, that's what you say. Courageous), and on the thrust of this misunderstanding I suddenly found myself catapulted behind her defences, so close to the stronghold of the self that I think it stunned us both. It was only a second, mind you, and I didn't press my advantage, nevertheless from that brief flash of intimacy I get the impression he's on the way out, that he's overstepped his limits this time, that the worm is turning.

And what a worm it is. A golden worm. A dragon with a hoard of treasures that the present keeper is too blind and ignorant to see. Not a compliment usually to call a woman a dragon but I mean it as such. A dragon is a strong, forthright, rather innocent creature, as I see it, unaware of its own strength, careless of its own peculiar brand of beauty. Solitary, shy, somewhat clumsy. Anachronistic, of course – totally out of place in the cramped modern world – but precious on that account too.

Dragon, dragon, burning bright. She said Blake's 'Tyger' was her favourite poem. What an awkward, jejune question to ask: What is your favourite poem? I don't know how I brought it over my lips without the censor lambasting me, but I did. And once she'd said it I knew that it was an absolutely inspired judgement, and when I got home I reached down from the shelf a sentimental Edwardian anthology that I haven't opened since childhood and read the whole thing out loud to myself and decided that, yes, it is indeed the greatest, loveliest piece of poetry ever written.

Wild, mad, preposterous even: words running amok like lunatics on a spree. She says it's a painter's poem and that's why she likes it so, because she can see the fires and the smoke and the forge and the stripes of the tiger as he comes red-hot off the tiger-smith's block, but to me it is above all and quintessentially a writer's poem. No thoughts to interfere, no meanings to distract, and the imagery is just an incidental spin-off: no, it is words in their naked ancestral state – sounds, beats, rhythms, playing on the deep, deep pulse that runs inside us all.

> Guido, I would that Lapo, thou, and I,
> Led by some strong enchantment, might ascend
> A magic ship, whose charmèd sails should fly . . .

A far cry from the 'Tyger' – a crystal chalice to an iron crucible – but she liked that too. I love the blanks in her education – art school has served her well in that respect; left her mind uncultivated, in strictly agrarian terms, but well tilled and fertile. A rich soil, a soil to grow things in; you get the impression that the pieces of information you cast on to it, provided they're vital enough in themselves, will find space, take root and flourish. I used to feel the same about Gaia's but have since come to the conclusion that hers is more like a deep freeze. She has boxes for things and labels to stick on them – Enlightenment thinker, Baroque composer, Secessionist painter and so forth, all very tidy and correct – but once she's done that she shelves them away and allows the frost to settle.

Too late now, of course, but I rubbish the educational system that taught me the points to look for in a woman and the points to ignore. I left school convinced I must shun the whole gender. The things I loved, the places I loved to visit in my imagination, lay inside the heads of other men, or so I thought; the rapturous fugues of childhood were still feasible, but only in the company of male friends, and only very few of them. Like Alice on the threshold of the magic garden, nibbling at her cake and swigging at her potion and telescoping uncontrollably from huge to tiny, I found access to my playground more and more difficult. Sex worked for a while as a key and then stopped working: with proper homosexuals it became too serious, with rogue ones like myself not serious enough. Orgasm was either sodden with drama or trivial like a sneeze; neither way did it feel right. When Lucy came along, with her girl/boy body and her charge of good-humoured, steamy but inconsequential eros, I was knocked senseless. No, sense-full. Not just a garden, I thought I'd found my way to blinking paradise. Never for a moment did I consider making a survey of the terrain, asking myself whether love could be built on it. I was like a savage with my first wristwatch – Patek Phillipe or Swatch, it was all the same to me. My father, with another of his sparing capsules of advice, bade me on a malicious note not to go ahead with the marriage until I had imagined to myself my future bride sitting on the loo. He seemed to regard this test as infallible and highly stringent, but for me it was useless. I had already seen Lucy on the loo, screwed with her in the loo, listened to her farts – she was a demon farter, probably still is, that's one aptitude age doesn't alter; in fact it was just this blend of sex and camaraderie that had bound me to her so fast in the first place.

What might have had more effect was if he had counselled me to watch her, as I did later on, prowling rapaciously through Peter Jones' basement department, cramming her trolley full of chintz-lined wastepaper bins. Or striding into a record shop, demanding the latest Aphrodite's Child LP. Or lying in bed in tears over some book about a woman who had tamed a lioness and lived to regret it. Or battling for tickets for *Hair*, or struggling into lurex leotards, or knocking back the sangria, or taking up astrology, or . . . Yes, maybe then I'd have paused and thought and said, Hang on, Henry, Aristophanes' theory in the Symposium is myth, OK, there are no missing halves, there are no seamless joins, but surely you could achieve a better fit than that?

With Gaia, on the other hand, the fit appeared instantly so snug that I should have realised it was merely due to her pliancy – tact, adaptive genius, call it what you will. She yielded, she gave, she poured into my spiky mould without leaving so much as a crack or an air bubble. She was living in London when I met her, from what I now appreciate was a deep contempt for the countryside and particularly the Italian countryside: within weeks of our wedding, there she was, touring rural Umbria in icy midwinter, house-hunting. She lists naturally towards trim upholstered furniture and tailored clothes: she decorated the house once she'd found it as if with the comfort of a pack of Labradors principally in mind, and has dressed ever since – I don't know how, but I've never seen anything on her twice which I've professed not to like at first wearing. Her favourite drink was and I think secretly remains Coca-Cola: she schooled herself in oenology for my sake and rapidly developed quite a sensitive palate. The books on my bedside table passed to hers, where they sojourned and still do for a congruous length of time – short ones briefly, long ones long. Like her father, Gaia can talk convincingly about anything for roughly the space of a meal: it is only when the meal for some reason is protracted, or when the topic is reintroduced at another sitting, that an attentive listener can pick up a slight ring of hollowness in her comments, and not always then.

There is a weekly publication in Italy – an institution, perhaps I should say – called *La Settimana Enigmistica*. A thickish little booklet packed full of verbal games and puzzles, with a graphic so peculiar as to be undatable. Crosswords abound: they are straightforward, unlike the English variety, but demand a familiarity with the classics that in a *Times* buff would be exceptional, and an even better memory. Name the seventh Muse, the eighth labour of Hercules, Alexander the Great's favourite pussycat, Cassandra's cousin twice removed – that sort of level. Gaia and her father used to race through it together like greyhounds, and even meretricious old Ma, with whom she does it now on the odd occasion, makes quite a good showing. Beyond the bare appellation their knowledge does not extend, but the proud pregnant names trip off their tongues like tiddlywinks and the booklet is discarded round about the Wednesday with all its spaces filled and hardly a correction in sight.

Oh, Henery, the sands are running out on you. Look into your shaving mirror and what do you see? The skull surfacing like jetsam at low tide from under a rapidly thinning layer of flesh: a few more millimetres and Bingo! It'll have gone the way of Yorrick's. You are not happy.

86

Gaia is not happy. You shudder to think that there is no other course for either of you than to hobble forward to the finish line the way you are doing now, hitched in ill-assorted tandem. You balk, you shy away, but *à quoi bon*? Like a beast at the treadmill, the future is plotted out for you and that is the road you will have to take.

*AMABILE – ARIA

If I had time – which I haven't – and if Don Filippo didn't have such terrible breath that comes through the grille at you like a whiff of fertiliser off the fields, I'd do well to go to confession this Sunday, as I've done a few things I'd like to get off my chest.

First I told a lie to the Avvocato. Well, it wasn't my fault, not entirely. He rang while Giovanna was out in the garden and I was inside on my own. Now she'd told me not to answer the phone – just let it ring and let the voice mail take over and only call her if it was Vicky from New Zealand or wherever it is – but habit is habit, and I was trying as usual to do too many jobs at once, so when I heard the ringing I picked up the receiver without thinking, and there was the Avvocato on the other end of the line.

He sounded a bit wrought up, emotional; called me by some funny pet name or other – something to do with a fox cub; must have mistaken my voice for Giovanna's. (People often do, which is curious because you'd think with her education and everything . . . but anyway they do, there was another man this morning, started gabbling at me in a foreign language and then rang off the moment I spoke. He sounded a bit wrought up too.)

'Oh, sorry, Amabile,' the Avvocato said, a little awkward, when I put him right. 'Can I speak to the Signora, please? Is she there?'

Lucky I didn't have to earn my bread in politics, I can't

tell a decent lie to save my neck. 'No, Avvocato,' I said. 'She isn't. She's gone . . . she's gone . . .' And then like a fool I stopped, as I couldn't think where to say, and to make things worse I could see Giovanna from where I was standing, looking up at the window, mouthing words at me and making signs, and it went quite against the grain to deceive him and keep the two of them apart. He may not be the right man for her, but he's her husband and Vicky's father, and all said and done I'd like to see the family stay united.

'Yes?' he said, sharpish, as if he could see Giovanna too, clear as daylight through the holes in the receiver, and knew I was covering up for her – taking her side against his. 'Where's she gone then?'

I hardly knew how to answer, I was in such a spot. Any old place would have done: out for a walk, round to a friend, down to the shops. But my brain was flapping about like a chicken under the chopper and the only thing that came into it for some daft reason was blackberries. There's a picture of them on the wall opposite the telephone, that must be why. So, she's gone picking blackberries, I said. Sounded half-baked.

'Oh,' he said. 'Blackberries, eh? Must have come early this year, Amabile. Isn't August the usual time?'

I could have kicked myself. But anyway he took pity on me in the end and let me off the hook. Just told me not to answer the next phone call because it would be him, leaving a message for Giovanna on the machine. 'If you *should* happen to see her, though,' he said as he hung up, in his real cunning lawyer's voice, 'tell her I rang, would you? Put in a good word for me.'

Not a dishonest action by today's standards – last week there was a man on the road to Foligno selling sheets that looked fine in the box, but when you went to unfold them there wasn't any material there, only the strip of turn-over backed by newspaper: caught half the village that way. In fact if I was to confess it to a priest as a sin, the man would probably tell me to buzz off and stop wasting his time. But as I said, I'm uncomfortable with untruths, and worse still when I get found out, and I'm not proud of myself at all.

The next thing was more serious: deliberate unkindness. Although the funny thing is, it bothers me less than the business with the Avvocato, and inside myself I'm still laughing. My brother brought his fancy Romanian girl-friend to have a meal with us on Sunday, and I spent the whole morning cooking. Fresh pasta, ragout, little tartlets with chicken livers, all the dishes he likes. Why go to the bother when I knew already the thanks I'd get for it? Well . . . because I said to myself, all right, she's only a raw young thing, and on the make, and probably half a gypsy too – they're nearly all gypsies in that part of the world according to Santino, who was there on a shooting trip last year – but still, he's taken a shine to her, my brother has, and it's the first time I've seen him perky in years, and he's growing old, and she keeps him company, and he isn't easy to get along with – moody as an old cur sometimes – and I'm his only family, so I'll put on a good show for him, I thought. Give a welcome to both of them. Do them proud.

The old lady sat there and watched me, never lifted a finger. Except once, and that was to tap it against her skull and tell me I needed my head examining. Never said a word either, all during the meal, but her eyes kept flashing sideways, missing nothing, taking it all in.

Rising ninety but she's closer on the ball than I am. It's a bad business, I'm afraid, whatever light you try to put on it. It drove a skewer through my stomach to see my poor old Bruno reduced to such a pass. He used to be the most sought-after bachelor in the whole village: nice car, good salary, house of his own, plenty of leisure time; only had to snap his fingers and he could have had any woman he liked. And now he's dancing round this little minx like a bear in the circus and she's the one to do the finger snapping. When we're married we'll have this, we'll have that. (Yes, it's marriage; she's out for the jackpot, won't settle for less, and that silly old Don Filippo keeps on putting his oar in, telling Bruno to make an honest woman of her. *That'd* take some doing!) A dishwasher, a microwave, a Jacuzzi – whatever that is, I don't think Giovanna's got one even, I must ask – a crystal coffee table, a spin dryer, a set of black china plates with underplates to match. You folks are countrified, you live in a backwater, you don't know what the market's got to offer. Treating us as if we were hobbledehoys off the fields and she was the princess, while if it wasn't for my poor old bamboozled brother she'd be whistling for her soup. He's bought her one of those pocket telephones already so she can call up her relatives: next thing they'll be coming over here in droves and he'll be supporting the lot of them.

Turned up her nose at all the food I'd prepared, didn't even pretend to eat some for politeness' sake. Didn't like oily dishes, didn't like heavy cooking, didn't like cheese, didn't like condiments. She's delicate, said my brother, trying to smooth things over, but you could tell it was done deliberately on her part, to disoblige. There she sat, chewing gum into our faces, and now and then you could see her stretch out her leg under the table in Bruno's direction and giggle, playing footsie or worse, and he'd go all glassy-eyed and giggle back. He never was all that bright, though he passed his surveyor's exams with a bit of coaching, but to see him now you'd think he'd scooped his brains clean out and fried them up for breakfast. Not a gram of sense left. I could hardly eat anything myself, I was so worried, thinking about the future: what she'll do when she's gone through the money; in what kind of a state she'll leave him; what he'll do when he's left on his own without her or it, and only us to take care of him.

I'd done various different sweets for afters, on Giovanna's advice – quite a selection – because she said we're a bit stuck into our nut-and-chocolate roll in these parts and young people are often slimming. The girl took one look and refused the lot of them: didn't like chocolate, didn't like liqueur, didn't like nuts, didn't like lemon, didn't like cream, didn't like ices . . .

And it was here that the old lady finally piped up. She never uses strong language as a rule, which made it all the more comic. 'You like a man's prick up your passage, Missie,' she said, really loud and clear. And fierce too, like a schoolmistress. 'That's all you like. Hah!' And then with a great cackle she was quiet again.

It was all over so quickly you'd hardly have known she'd spoken, but the words no, they sort of stayed there. And after a moment of nobody knowing what to say or do, we started laughing. Me first, I'm afraid, and then the old woman herself, and then Beppe, and finally my brother and – just a little bit, to do her justice – the girl as well. It did us a world of good, it cleared the air, it brought us closer together. In the long run it won't make the least jot of difference – she'll still fleece him and break his heart and give us a lot of headaches too while she's about it – but at least, with that one good honest lash of my mother-in-law's, she knows now that we're not taken in by her. And that makes it somehow easier to bear.

Third and last thing was extravagance, but I'm so ashamed of that I can hardly mention it, not even to myself. I'm not an easy target for postal offers as a rule, I don't know what came over me. The business of the girl must have made me envious, that's what: I kept looking at her nails with the pearly lacquer on them and not a chip to be seen, and thinking how long it'd last on mine. Anyway, I've signed the paper now so there's no going back. Sixteen volumes – gold lettering, dark-red covers just like leather, beautiful presentation case to keep them in, and all that knowledge inside that puts your portable phones and whatnots to shame. It'll come in handy for the boys' homework too, as long as they don't touch it with greasy fingers. How I shall tell Beppe I daren't think, but I'll start worrying about that when the first package arrives. A – ARVI, ARVO – BRACCI. Sounds beautiful too.

*ORSO MARIA AND ANSWERPHONE — DUET

– Thanks for calling. Please leave a message after the beep.

– Joanna? Giovanna? Are you there? Where are you? Are you out? Listen, Giovanna, please, if you are there . . . Oh, hang, never mind. You aren't there, are you? No, well . . . Never mind, I'll ring later.

– Thanks for calling. Please leave a message after the beep.

– Giovanna? Joanna? Volpetta? Volpettina? If you're there please answer. Are you there? Giovanna, don't behave like this. At least let me talk, let me explain . . . Giovanna? Giovanna? Oh, it's no use . . .

– Thanks for calling. Please leave a message after the beep.

– Giovanna? It's evening, I know you're there. Listen. Listen to me, please. I'm not coming, OK. Don't worry, I respect your choice, I know you don't want to see me and I'm not going to force you or anything . . . Giovanna, I can't talk to you like this. And I must talk to you. I spoke to Vicky today – no, it's nothing to do with Vicky, she's fine – I just need to talk to you, that's all. Ring me, OK? *Please.*

EMILY — RECITATIVE IN E-MAIL

charlotte_porterhouse@virgin.net

july 11th?

porker how's things god it's boring here and god it's hell being pregnant in this heat last summer at least i could get stoned now and again when i was desperate but with a fetus – there's a letter missing there somewhere but whatever i put looks wrong – in your belly somehow you can't then I'll have to breast-feed until the brat's practically voting age because my doctor's such a bully about things like that and by the time i'm through i'll probably have lost the taste old age responsibility groan :-)

had a long talk about all this with poor old henry last night depressed me no end i mean he really is rolling into the terminus so what can you say send me some decent mags if you get time to keep my spirits up don't go in for unsafe sex my porkerina is my closing advice because it can COST YOU DEAR love and xxxs

e

JOANNA — ARIA

I remember when I was in my last year of school reading a novel about a sexy, glamorous concert pianist with dozens of menfriends, and getting all involved in the story, and then being brought up short by discovering that the heroine was all of thirty-five. It seemed indecent, someone of that venerable age still being involved in the traffic of love.

Little did I suspect that I would still be shunting around in it myself much further down the line. Orso rang three times today – maybe even more if I count the times the answerphone kicked in and then beeped with no message. What does that mean? At the very, very least that he is trying to get in touch with me for reasons he doesn't like to leave recorded. Not parcels of books, therefore. Not to tell me I've got a parking fine or warn me that my car licence is about to expire. And what effect does it have on me, his nudging into my orbit again?

Unfortunately, whatever it is, it's a strong one. Could be fear, could be hope, could be longing, could be revulsion, I honestly can't say, but it plucks at my nerves worse than a plectrum and interferes with my work and does something to my digestion as well. Like a hunted animal of long experience I hold my breath and attune my ears and say to myself, Here he comes, the man with the bait that lures and weapons that wound. What's he up to this time? What's he brought with him? What's his game? How long is he going to play it for? How long before he gives up and goes away?

Only certainty, only query which doesn't even need posing, so definite is the answer, is that this time, no matter what he says or does, I will not walk back into the jaws of his trap. At long last I have gnawed myself free, and the agony it cost me to do so cannot, must not, have been suffered in vain. (But even as I say that the metaphor switches and instead of wary prey, there I am, a fawning hunting dog: Then he's *coming back*; wag tail, slobber tongue, *Master's coming back*.)

Get a hold of yourself you flabby Labrador, you spineless spaniel. If he does come back, he'll have to go away again, and that's all there is to it. I virtually said as much to Vicky over the phone last night in order to prepare her. She seemed quite unfazed, but then her generation hop in and out of partnerships with the ease of square-dancers: dozy do and take another spin. Untrendy nowadays to suffer much for love. 'It may take you a bit of getting used to,' was all she said, as if being single again after twenty odd years was on a par with breaking in a new pair of flip-flops. 'But think of the perks. You needn't cook any more, you can go and see all the films in English, you can paint when you feel like it instead of having to fit it round Papà's court hearings.' Then went on to tell me she and Leonardo had been bungee jumping. 'For me it's going to be more like that, the separation – a bungee jump into the void,' I said, not quite so nimble in my change of theme. Ah, yeah, sure, bound to be, well, that was fun too once you got past the first lurch.

She's probably right, but am I past the first lurch? I'd like to think so – I *did* think so. Only now, as I replay the messages minus earplugs and listen to that familiar persuasive voice with the unfamiliar note of urgency in it, I'm no longer sure. My friend and next-door neighbour Claudia, who is something of an expert in these things, having been divorced twice, suggested I start packing Orso's things away – preferably in black dustbin sacks, which are spacious and cheap and gratifyingly offensive as well. Hang on to the suitcases, she advised, you can always change the initials; and store the sacks in the garage so you don't have to be there when he comes to collect them. OK, it's probably not the sort of thing I could ever bring myself to do – far too drastic and Latin – but why is it I haven't even moved one material object to underline the new state of affairs between us? I don't know – made my bed up single, for example, or taken full possession of the dressing table or thrown his toothbrush away?

Too busy? Well, there is that as well of course. Maybe, with the exhibition looming, I should never have accepted this scenery job of Henry's because he's a far harder task master than I'd thought. Keeps ringing at odd times during the day to ask how things are coming on and how far I've got and whether I've found all the props and whatnots, and whether I need money or help to go and fetch them. If he was an Italian I might even suspect he had something other than stage management in mind. But with him, so upper crust and bookish – donnish is more the word I'm looking for – it seems rather vulgar to think along these lines. In fact I can't really associate him with sex at all. That stoop, those shoulders, that elongated El Greco look – I wonder how Gaia manages in the bedroom? For me it would be slightly like screwing a cardinal. (Or perhaps I mean an archbishop, because if I remember rightly from school cardinals don't necessarily have to be priests. But anyway, whichever. A churchman, a dignitary, someone who makes you feel that all bodily functions are reprehensible and rather naff.) Besides, he's simply too old for someone of my age. Once you're past forty you get choosy in that respect, I find. Familiar oldies are all right because you remember them young, and their younger self is still there, legible, under the wrinkles, but new oldies, no, they won't do at all.

I'm flattered though. And more than flattered: I'm pleased. I discover that for some reason or other I love talking to him. I wonder why? Normally I wouldn't have time for a posh old codger like him, but his mind is posh too, which sorts of elevates the poshness to a different plane. Quite what I mean by that I'm not sure, but I think I mean that he's got a really elegant, accomplished way of displaying the contents of his head. He talks so prettily, as if talking was an art and not just – like it is with me – a mental equivalent to crapping and getting things out of my system. He takes trouble over his words, he interests me, he stimulates me, he makes me pause over mine. Above all he makes me laugh. In a way that Orso never did or does or would ever be able to. Orso tells jokes, but they are bracketed jokes, set apart from the rest of his conversation, while with Henry the laughs are dovetailed into the whole, so that in listening to him you are carried along on a joyride: up and down and fast and slow and round corners into unexpected places – all fun to visit. If the physical spark worked between us as well – cor! I would be in trouble, but it doesn't, so that simplifies things.

Amabile, however, bless her, definitely thinks there's

something fishy in all these calls, and the odd thing is, after all her egging me on to be independent and snap my fingers in Orso's face, she's now swung the other way and is standing up for him. 'It's that man again,' she says in a mildly disapproving voice, every time she gets Henry on the phone. 'That foreigner. I told him the Avvocato wasn't here but he says he doesn't want to talk to the Avvocato, he wants to talk to you.'

'He's calling about the play,' I reassure her. 'The opera we're putting on in Montaldo.'

But she stays sceptical. 'Ah, yes, the opera,' she says. 'So that's what they call it now – opera!' And then lingers by the telephone, dusting, her head tilted on one side like the HMV terrier, trying to see if I act flustered – reading my body language since the other is closed to her.

When I've finished she usually makes some generalised remark, aimed, I think, chiefly at protecting me, but not only me. Men are all the same the world over. Not to be trusted. After one thing and one thing only. Worse than tomcats on the prowl. And once they've got it they're off without so much as a thank you. A hair of a woman's crotch pulls stronger than a team of oxen, so they say in these parts, but not for long, oho, not for long.

When I laugh she relaxes. Yesterday, on her way out, she stopped in the sitting room for a moment and looked about her as if she were a visitor, eyeing the furniture, pictures and knick-knacks whose layout she knows even better than I do. 'If anything should change in this house,' she said, 'it would be a blow to me. I know it's too much to ask, but I'd like things here to remain for ever just as they are. You know what I mean, Giovanna.'

I know what she means. I had the same feeling once, years ago, piercingly, when Vicky was about six. She and Orso had had the measles together and we came here in the early spring for them to recuperate. I was in the kitchen, getting food for them, and they were sitting outside in a shaft of sunlight doing a jigsaw puzzle, with their heads close together, and this beautiful music was pouring out into the garden – I think it was *Don Giovanni* again, in fact I'm sure it was: Zerlina's song to Masetto as she promises to heal him of his bruises, *Vedrai, carino*. And I was watching them from the window, and the Judas tree was in flower, and the words of the aria seemed to express my feelings for both of them so perfectly that – I don't know – it was just as if everything in the universe in that brief slice of time was in its rightful place. Total happiness, total well-being, all the good stars aligned, if only I could hold them so. Then in my trance I set fire to the pan holder and by the time I'd put the flames out the sun had gone in again, and that was that, and the moment had passed. But for ages afterwards I couldn't help feeling that if only I'd been more careful with the flame of the gas . . .

Stupid. Life flows and you've got to go with it. Beaver dam-work gets you nowhere, only tires you out and gives you rheumatism from being so long in the wet. I want to enjoy myself in a restful sort of way from now on, insofar as this is possible. No more peaks, but no more valleys. And no more bloody ravines like the one I've just climbed out of. What do I need Orso for? What do I need any man for? Sex? Financial security? Company? I've got my work, I've got my friends, I've got my middle finger – I'm laughing.

I said Orso's approach interferes with my work. The verb

is not quite right: it influences my work, which is slightly different. Artists have that up their sleeve, that whatever happens, however badly someone messes around with them, they can turn it into material. Orso draws blood: half of me says, Ow! and the other says, Ah, rusty red, just the shade I was looking for. I worked on E4 last night, after listening to the messages, and the paint came off my brush alive, vibrating – all the tension in me going straight on to the canvas. In placid periods I often get bogged down, lose my sense of direction, and have to stumble on until the sheer dissatisfaction with what I'm doing creates its own brand of tension. In a way, artistically speaking, that's more painful still. A kind of self-flagellation. With someone else doing the beating, at least your whip arm is free.

You're not easy to live with, you know, Orso said to me once, defending himself for some minor escapade with a female who, vice versa, according to him, was easiness made flesh. And maybe he's right, maybe I'm not, maybe no artist ever is. Maybe they – we – should never tie ourselves to a partner at all. Have children, yes, why not, children are another form of artistic product, but not link up our lives to that of another unrelated adult. Maybe, if you look at it closely, it is we, not the Orsos of this world, who are the great egoists.

Yes, Amabile would say to that, and maybe that political porno star Cicciolina is a virgin. Dear Ami, I must go down and see her now. She left a slightly worked-up message on the machine too: I'm afraid there's some trouble brewing with that dotty daughter-in-law.

HENRY — ARIA

The world is fathomless. Human beings are extraordinary. Life is extraordinary. I went to bed last night feeling a hundred and one and ready for the knacker's and this morning I wake up in love and round about sixteen.

It is also extraordinary – or maybe it isn't – that the first reaction to this new state of being should be so self-centred, so selfish almost. Do I think of the other person involved? Yes, of course I do, and have done so constantly, from the moment my feet touched the floor and, like the songwriters say, found air underneath the soles instead. (My head is ringing with popular songs all of a sudden. What *is* the censor doing? Off on holiday, I expect. About time. Stuffy old turd, long may he remain there.) Jo*anna*, I warble to the Bernstein music, Jo*anna*, Jo*anna*, I'll never stop saying Jo*anna*. But really she doesn't interest me, not yet, not in herself – only as a litmus test to apply to *me* and wonder at the effects she causes. What will happen next, when I will next see her, what I shall say to her when I do, how and whether I shall declare my passion and how and whether she will respond – all this lies suspended in the Leibnizland of possible events while I probe in delight and amazement at the rusty but still functioning mechanism of my heart. It works. It feels. It expands and contracts with hope and despair like a squeeze box. I can scarcely credit it. Next thing and I'll be having a morning erection that holds good *after* I've peed.

I love Gaia again, I love this beautiful place we live in. Our housekeeper is wreathed in light like a figure of Vermeer as she pours out my coffee – never noticed before what graceful forearms she has. Emi, slouched over the breakfast table in a grubby peignoir, appears to me like a vision of the Madonna. Morning, 'enry. Morning, my sweet, my sweet. (Don't blink at me like that. I'm not sick, I'm just in lo-ove.) I take the stairs in threes – arthritis of the ankle? Can't remember what it is. I skate to the upstairs telephone, rucking up the carpet on the landing in an attempt to see how far I can slide, and summon those involved in the production to an evening rehearsal with follow-up pizza in the square – all except Joanna, whose magical voice in my ear I store up for later. I dance down again, waltz into my study, clap shut the books I have been reading – who needs books on a day like this? Musty old things, bad for the eyesight – and merrily dispatch all the daunting paperwork that has been accumulating on my desk over the past weeks. I sign my cheques with such *élan* I wonder for a moment if my bank will query the signature: they did once, last summer, when Emi got me going on pot. But this is different: I soar, and yet my head is clear as aspic. From my high quota I can see myself – greying, balding, unlovely, unmuscular, capering around like a colt, a figure to the gods of such absurdity that if indeed they have devised us for their sport they must be splitting their divine sides.

But I see myself with equal clarity as a victor too. It can't be otherwise. I feel the whole weight of English literary creation behind me. I ride Blake's Tyger; I surge through the air on the wings of Tennyson's Eagle. My love is in exile and I will fetch her home; she is starved of the words of her native tongue and I will feed her them. (Strong silent men, my arse! Watch what this weak loquacious type can do.) I will chat her up with Chatterton, woo her with Wyatt, kiss her with Keats. I will stun her with Donne and marvel her with Marvell . . .

No, there go the gods guffawing again, I will of course do nothing of the kind. But what I mean is that, whatever it is, and if it *is* anything beyond the lettering on a passport, I have Englishness on my side. St George is with me (forget for a moment that he was Roman like the foe) and will help me win my dragon. It's no contest at all really. What can that sodding Volpi marshal, beyond his Porsche and his tan and his fading gigolo charm? Nothing. Even if he wanted to hang on to her – which is unlikely: in the set he mingles with I should think wives are thrown out of the window regularly on New Year's Eve together with the washing machine and the telly; youth is all, newness is all. But. Just say that for sentimental reasons he did want to hang on to her, what other weapons could he possibly deploy? Not to boast, but I am wiser and better bred and better read and better connected and better company and more patient. Richer too, which never hurts. I am also far, far kinder. Gentler. All round a nicer man.

Kind? Nice? Gentle, Henry? What about your proposed behaviour towards Gaia? How does that fit in with this description?

Woah, wait a moment. To start with I am not proposing to alter my behaviour towards Gaia in any way as yet, except to be kinder to her as well. I *am* kinder already, if you haven't noticed. Reason with me closely: what have I done to her so far except bore her stiff, deny her children, keep her stranded in the country half the year round and disappoint her thoroughly, both as a writer and a man? Very little, no? Virtually nothing? So, what would I do to her if I were to leave her? Would I damage her? Hurt her? Spoil her life for her? Maybe, just a little, to begin with, but in the long run I would simply be setting her free, striking off her shackles for her that tie her to this ill-suited old crock that is me. Especially if I were to leave her soon, now, while she is still young and strong and beautiful and capable of making a new – better – beginning. From afar, more like a father than a husband, I could watch over her, see that she lacks nothing in the material line, all in all make her much happier than I do now. And then – her rubber constitution: she would bounce back from the upset like an acrobat off a trampoline. Oh, no, I am brooding no ill against Gaia, far from it.

Besides, she doesn't really love me, and probably never has. She loves the things that go with me – the chic, the kudos, the social perch they enable her to attain. Absurd in someone so young, but the title – she loves that too. She is a snob, I'm afraid, poor love, in the faintly damning sense my parents used to give to the word: their generation snobbed snobs, snobs were not the thing to be at all.

Oh, God, I'm so happy. Failed all round, useless parasitic member of the human race, my energies currently employed on nothing weightier than a village fête, and I'm as busy and fulfilled as Kanga on a vest count. Shelve the High Renaissance and romantic literature for a sec, think of having a life companion reared on *Winnie the Pooh*. So amusing, the *orsetto Pu*, would be what Gaia would say. Pooh Bear is

not amusing, he is hilarious, rapturous, nauseating, obnoxious, masterly, depending on your taste, but for a whole
elderly wedge of English population he is a formative force
to be reckoned with. For my mother, for example, he was a
paragon, a role model: her reactions to practically all the
significant events of her life were based on what her ursine
hero would have said or done in similar circumstances. At
weddings, after funerals, in all moments of high drama –
she was even known to have said it during the war while
crouched in the cellar in the throes of an air raid: Well,
everyone, how about a little something? Pressed for an
opinion on any subject bar gardening, where modesty went
to the wind: I am a woman of ve'y little brain. Most
crushing verdict of all, far exceeding the accusation of
snobbery: Needs a little unbouncing, don't yer think?
And so on.

What she said in the sack I dread to contemplate, but I'll
be buggered if some of her philosophy hasn't rubbed off on
me as well, because guess what's going through my poor
old agitated noddle now? How sweet to be a cloud, floating
in the blue . . . *Non v'è cosa peggior*, goes the Neapolitan
proverb, *che in vecchie membra sentir il pizzicor d'amore*.
Nothing worse than to feel the itch of love in an old body. I
disagree entirely. My old body has never felt better, nor has
the cranky old pump inside.

*ORSO MARIA – SERENADE TO A MOBILE PHONE

Ehi? Piccolina? Orso. Look, I'm sorry. This case is turning into a real nightmare. Yesterday the hearing dragged on so long I had to skip supper entirely. Me, dining alone at midnight on frozen pasta – can you picture your poor Orsone? I'm the one who should be complaining, not you. Go to the sea by all means – do you good, and I love to see you brown, reminds me of Sardinia. No work over the weekend, so I'll ring you early Saturday morning, then, OK? Bring you croissants for your breakfast and plant kisses on your little sunburnt nose.

* AMABILE – ARIA

Lucia is in hospital in Montefalco – I've just been over there to take her some fruit and clean nighties. Fracture of the thighbone, the doctors say. But that's not the worrying thing, the bone will mend. The worrying thing is that they found drugs on her in the car – enough, according to the Maresciallo, to get her sent to prison for drug pedalling.

I'm not sure it isn't the worst thing that's happened to us yet. The death of a son is so terrible there's no words for it, but it's clean, if you know what I mean. You can hold your head up, talk about it to other people, even discuss it with the children. This thing, no, you have to keep it hidden like a dirty disease.

There is no God, I'm sure of that now. He'd have had to create the stuff, wouldn't he, and what sort of a God would go and create heroin? And on what day of the week? The Saturday, ready for the disco round?

Who was she going to sell it to, that's what I keep wondering? She's got sons of her own – whose sons and daughters was she going to go and sell it to?

Oh, Lucia, Lucia. It's my fault too, I ought to have done something sooner, not just waited for this. You can't do anything, Giovanna said, and I believed her. But it was cowardice, weakness, laziness that stopped me acting. I should have gone to the Carabinieri weeks ago, that's what I should have done, and denounced Lucia and begged them to take her in on any pretence. Anything to get her off the streets and into a place like a hospital or a community centre, where there's people who could have helped her properly, professionally, knowing what they were doing.

Now it'll be prison, and by the time she comes out we'll have lost her. I keep thinking of Stefano looking down from wherever he is and banging his fists the way he used to when he was really het up about something and begging me to step in for him and set things straight. Only then I think he's only got clouds to bang them on, so he can't be doing that. And then it strikes me that, if there's no God, there's no heaven and no clouds and no Stefano either, and I feel even lonelier and more at a loss as to what to do.

Beppe's flipped over the top. Whatever I say he just looks at the floor, and then says he's got to go out and mend the jeep. He's been tinkering with it almost non-stop ever since the call came from the police – tap, tap, tap, the noise of that spanner drives me wild. I have trouble stopping myself from shouting out of the window at him something I'd regret. Giovanna was right about that at least: in a fix it's we women who have to find the strength somewhere.

The old lady's strong all right, but it takes her differently. She just sets her mouth and flicks on the telly and says Lucia was a no-gooder from the start. That boy of ours spoilt her, she says. Central heating. Washing machines. In her day a young woman worth her salt had to fetch the wood and carry the water and scrub the clothes at the village pump along with all the other wives. Didn't have time for drugs then, you were lucky if you got half a cigarette and half a minute to smoke it in between chores. The boys won't just be all right, they'll be a darn sight better off without a mother like that messing around in the background. I'm to stop fretting and let the law take its course. Once the girl's inside, she says, at least we'll know where she is. And as for the village people and the gossip – let them talk till their tongues drop off. There's not one of them can set themselves up as a preacher, she's known them all from the cradle and the pickles they got into, and if anyone should try she'll pay them back in the same coin. It's a small place but – oho! the things these old eyes of hers have seen.

I've said nothing to the boys yet. Lucia took a knock against the windshield too and the bruise on the forehead has spread half the way down her face, and I don't want them to see her until it's gone down a bit: I don't even want them to see her in hospital or know she's there. They can sense something's up, though, and they're nervous as hares. Hardly fight at all any more: just sit together on the sofa, reading comics, each one for himself, and every time the telephone rings you can see them hold their breath and go so still it's unnatural. Tonight I'll say something, tell them half the truth perhaps, to reassure them, but I'm afraid if I mention the words car accident it'll have a terrible effect, especially on Mario. Maybe I'd better say she's having her tonsils out or something. But then they'll want to see her, and if I say they can't, then they'll take fright again and . . .

Anyway, I'll work it out with Joanna when she drops by. I'm sorry I haven't been able to get over to help her today – there was the carpenter coming for the shutters and he always leaves the place like a stable – but the driving back and forth to the hospital makes it difficult. It seems funny, her doing things for me instead of the other way round, but she insisted on doing my shopping as well when she went to do hers, and I'm that pushed I couldn't refuse. The hospital food's terrible: I'd like to get some substance into that daft girl, if only for Stefano's sake, so I thought I'd run her over some chicken broth with pasta in the afternoon. Her mother was there in the ward when I arrived this morning, and what do you think she'd brought? A lace bed shawl and a fancy image of the Madonna, all done in pearls, to hang over the bed and impress the other patients.

I told the old lady. I'll give her lace, she said, and I'll give her pearls, and I'll give her the Madonna too. Never had anything in the top storey, the women in that family. A good lawyer's what they need now, silly magpies, not a picture of the blessed Virgin. Paugh! And then she pulled herself out of her chair and – wonder of wonders – went and did the dishes for me. And when she'd finished she took me into her room and pressed some money on me she's been setting aside from her pension. For the lawyer, she said, and if any's left over, you keep it, Ami. You're a good daughter-in-law, couldn't have asked for a better, you deserve it.

Nearly had me crying. It wasn't much of course – old people seem to lose touch with the value of money, I've noticed that before, always in their own favour too – but it was the words, the gesture. It showed that underneath that leathery cover she cares and understands.

And speaking of leathery covers, the post office in Perugia sent a card today to say there's a parcel there for me for collection. It's the books, the first instalment, but I think now, what with this new drain on our finances, I'll just have to ring up the firm that sells them and cancel the whole thing. Hope they don't turn nasty: that's all we need now – the police after me as well.

*GAIA – ARIA, AND CAVATINA
FINALE WITH LAPTOP

Life is so full of surprises you can never get bored. I said that
this evening to Henry, when we were all sitting round the
table in the square having supper after the rehearsal, and
instead of curling his mouth at me the way he does when I
make a commonplace remark – and I do, I'm afraid, quite
often, and this was one of them: I haven't got the English
knack for sparkly anecdote – he took my hand and
squeezed it and said in a kind of sad but happy voice,
Yes, my darling love, how right you are.

All is well between us again. The cloud or whatever it was
has vanished, melted away in this wonderful summer
sunshine. What heat this year – I love the heat. And what
fun this acting business is, and how pretty the music is when
you get to know it and are able to recognise when the
melodies are coming up: the score is full of melodies, many
more than I thought.

This evening we were a proper team, and I think for the
first time everyone started to realise it, and to feel we're
involved in something – oh, another commonplace, but
never mind – something bigger than ourselves. There's no
proper lighting yet, of course, and no amplifiers and no
costumes, and Isobel Marcucci had a sore throat and had to
be replaced for the evening by Henry's pal Joanna, who
luckily knew the part but couldn't act to save her hefty
neck; and Masetto and I still need a bit of prompting, and

endless little things were missing and went wrong and there were hold-ups every two minutes, but all the same there was a sense of achievement, of getting somewhere, of something, as I said, rather special and surprising coming into being.

Henry didn't take us all the way through, he stopped us at the scene just before the cemetery, where Elvira is on stage alone and sings that warbly bit, *Mi tradì quell'alma ingrata* – or however it goes. And very sweetly, seeing how tired I was, he asked Joanna if she wouldn't mind stepping in for me too, which she did, although you could tell she didn't really want to. (And can you wonder? Henry is a bit unperceptive that way, I'm afraid. I've told him over and over again about the husband, but he *keeps* on forgetting.) And when we'd finished – and as I said there was no scenery or action or anything, only Madame Carabiniere in her baggy trousers mouthing along in playback – but when we'd finished the whole square remained absolutely still for a moment like the castle of the Sleeping Beauty: even the card players interrupted their game; and then there was a sort of silent sigh as everyone came back to life. And I looked at Henry, who was looking at the stage, and he seemed so carried away and happy I couldn't help feeling the same, since I haven't seen him like that for months. No, perhaps even longer than months. At the start I disapproved of the whole business thoroughly, but now I have to admit it's doing him good to have this sideline, this hobby. After all, whatever people say, writing is not quite like other work, in the sense that other activities don't necessarily distract you from it. In fact, quite the reverse, they may distract you *to* it. (See, Gaia, you too are capable of original ideas when you put your mind to it. I'm sure nobody ever told me that, I just thought it up for myself this very instant.) I don't want to speak too soon, but Henry shut himself in his study when we got in after the supper, and I think, I *think*, I heard him opening the drawer where he keeps the printed draft of the novel and then clicking away on his computer ... So, we shall see. I have a great hankering to just take a tiny peep at the manuscript to make sure, but if he found me at it, he might feel I was putting pressure on him, and all the benefits might be lost. It's no easy matter, being the partner of a writer: you have to think of all these things. And you have to be very observant too, and very sensitive.

Misa,
Tear up that silly mopey letter I wrote you a little while back. All is well now, can't think what got into me, must be hormones. Henry is out of his depression or whatever it was, and the cloud between us has passed. Maybe there never was one even, maybe it was all in my head, but if there was one it's gone, melted in this wonderful summer sunshine. I think – I'm not sure, but I think he's even taken up his writing again, which with him is the best possible sign. His proper writing, I mean. His novel.

Thank your lucky stars, *Misetta mia*, that you're married to a commodity broker. At least you know the cause of his ups and downs! Long to see you and have a proper, proper talk. So glad London is on.

Kisses, G.

*JOANNA AND
MOBILE PHONE – TRIO

– Omnitel. The subscriber of this number is not at present available. Your call is being transferred to an answer service. Please hold the line.

– You have reached the answer service of the number 0348/774/4903. If you wish you may leave a short message after the tone. Beep.

– Orso, it's me, Joanna. Look, I'm not calling about us, OK. Get that straight, nothing's changed, I don't want to see you, I still don't want to see you, but I need to talk to you. The thing is, Amabile's in trouble. Her daughter-in-law – Stefano's widow, you remember, the one with the nice figure who used to bring the kids over to swim – she's had a car accident and . . . Oh, God, it's a bit complicated, I don't even like saying it over the phone . . . but anyway, if you could just call me this evening, the moment you get time . . . Thanks. Bye. No, sorry, don't call me, call Amabile direct. Better. I may be a bit late back.

*ORSO MARIA AND
ANSWERPHONE — DUET

– Thanks for calling. Please leave a message after the beep.
  – Giovanna? Fox cub? Old companion of mine? What is
this? I am worried. Where are you? What are you up to,
staying out so late at night? Listen, this is stupid, you say
you need to talk to me, and now I can't find you. I need to
talk to you too. And not about Amabile or anyone, I need to
talk to you about yourself, about me, about our life
together. I have never believed . . . You must try to understand . . . I have never . . . Oh, ring me, my sweet fox cub,
the moment you get back, no matter what time it is. Please,
please, I implore you . . .

HENRY — ROMANCE AND ARIA

That evening for Napier signalled a watershed, a demarcation line between two eras. Eras that another man might cursorily have labelled in his mind, BT and AT: Before Then and After Then, but that Napier himself, always precise about such things, preferred to think of as Before Then and Anno Traditionis – the year of his surrender.

Christ, that BT looks bad. Have to do something about it, but later, so as not to interrupt the flow.

It was a question of control. Until that evening, and more exactly until the infinitesimal time-slice of that evening during which the line was drawn, the rational part of his brain, whatever it consisted in and wherever it was lodged, had presided over the emotional. Like a scientist observing an experiment, it had stood there at its mental microscope, watching, calculating, taking notes, occasionally smiling, occasionally frowning, occasionally scratching its head in surprise, but all the while detached and indisputably in command. Then, suddenly, the change, the Gestalt switch, the vindication of the Heisenberg principle, and this rational element had been whisked by the hem of its white laboratory overall under the lens, on to the slide, just another passive participant among the rest. It could still see itself, still take note, and to some extent still frown and smile and wonder too at what it saw, but it could no longer do anything to alter things: its power had gone; it had taken a purler.

Purler? That must be grotesquely dated by now. It sounds dated even to me. Where the hell does it come from anyway? Knitting, says my dictionary. *Knitting*? Ah, yes, I remember my mother's post-war socks and the speed with which a stitch, one dropped, used to plummet to the border – unstoppable, irretrievable, vanishing into the dense black hole of the casting-on. But why a purler, then? Why not a plainer? Because the purls were more droppable than the plains, that's why. I know this for a fact: I was made to post-war-knit too, together with my sister Grizzle – Griselda, Emi's mother. I was rather better at it than she was, I rather liked it. I excelled at crochet: in my first term at prep school I held crochet classes, which we all regarded for a while as what Emi would term cool, until brutally disabused by our elder companions . . .

Some flow, Henry. You don't want to write, do you? You are charged like a rocket on the launch pad and yet you don't want to write. You want to live, that's what. *O vivere o scrivere*, says that Italian novelist pal of Gaia's, you either write or you live. Dreadful ponce, but it's perfectly true. And I opt for the *vivere*. Napier – what a sodawful, God-awful name. Gaia's gone up to bed already but I don't want to follow her, I want to put the Busch version of *Don Giovanni* on the record player and turn it up to blast force and stroll out into the night with a glass of Brachetto in my hand, and lie myself flat on the ground with my nose to the stars and relish just being who I am, where I am, in the turmoil that I am.

. . . its power had gone; it had conked out / come a cropper / gone for a burton.

All desperately outmoded. Is ruin no longer fashionable, or what? Let's try aeronautics.

. . . its power had gone; it had taken a nose-dive.

Dam-buster stuff, but it'll have to stand. And who cares anyway. I'm turning to the Brachetto now, which ages better than language.

Napier. Napier and his nose-dive – good luck to the bastard. Perhaps I should never have set her there on the stage in that last scene. Perhaps it was selfish of me, but I couldn't resist, just for those brief few minutes, placing her in the role in which she belongs. It doesn't matter that on the night of the performance Gaia's cat-like grace will replace her poignant clumsiness, that instead of the rugged pathos of a late Rodin we will have a neat little Capodimonte shepherdess, all flounce and lightness, it doesn't matter. All that matters is that I have seen her the way I wanted to see her from the outset, and have lost my heart. The way I also presumably wanted to lose it from the outset.

What can love be? Where can its sweetness lie? Analyse this wine and you will strike fructose, like as not, but fell me down this instant and carry out a post-mortem and there will be nothing in my carcass to testify the blissful state I'm

131

in tonight. Unless of course, rather than ingredients, it is a question of organisation. Who knows? Perhaps to some brain specialist of the future my head would present an easy read. Look at this old geezer here, he might well say to his students: classic case of senile besottedness; all the neurones ranged in bliss-pattern, not one out of line. Yep, this specimen was on a sentimental high all right when he kicked the bucket.

That there *is* an underlying rational and material explanation for all our emotions, love included, is a belief that I cling to – in desperation, I think, in the manner that the drowning man is supposed to cling to his proverbial straw. So as not to drown without at least putting up a tiny formal rag-end flutter of resistance. Glug, struggle, glug. As I see it, we humans are organisms perpetually torn asunder by the dual demands of self and society. We are social beings with social needs that pursue us like Furies unless fulfilled, and at the same time we are isolated fastnesses that collar all resources for internal consumption and practise strictest autarky out of greed and fear. What a fix. What a crucifixion. No accident that the figure of the dying Christ caught on in the public imagination: his plight is our plight, his mode of death our mode of life – a continuous racking of the self in two contrasting directions: thither, to the outside world, and hither, to good old number one.

Then what happens? As we lie there twisted on our several crosses, bibbity bobbity boo and along comes love, and for its duration and thanks to the sleight of heart it works in us, the tension is resolved: we blend with another being. Greed and fear are placated: we nourish and give out

132

and are generous and sociable, and no worry, because all along it is ourselves we are feeding and ourselves with whom we are having commerce. We feel good because we are good. Or we *seem* good, because in reality, as in the tube of a kaleidoscope, it is all done with mirrors. Our borrowed self holds up a glass to us, and we hold one back to it, and the two of them – or the two of us, that is – gaze enraptured at the suite of images it reflects. Look at me giving, we shrill, delighted, look at me . . .

Fuck. Worse than my mother. I don't seem to be able to develop any serious thought without the intrusion sooner or later of A. A. Milne. Look at me philosophising in the vocabulary of Roo. Look at me droning on with the spurious erudition of that blasted strigiform. Look at me making an all-time Eeyore of myself. The whole course of thought is idle anyway, because even if the above argument is valid it, A, changes nothing in the way I feel, thank God, and B, applies only to reciprocated love, whereas I have no idea whether mine is or isn't.

Oh, Christ in Heaven. Why did I ever loose that thought, why did I let it slither to the surface? Is it? Or isn't it? Does she or doesn't she? End of comfy solipsistic phase and back to the torture chamber. How can I lounge here cradling my Brachetto without having addressed this basic question on which all my happiness, as I see so clearly now, depends? How can I pass the night? How can I sleep or even pretend to? How can I so much as draw another tranquil breath?

The telephone? No, you fool, the telephone is out as a medium for lovesick quinquagenarians. The telephone will only do for adolescents. I cannot adopt a plastic mouthpiece as a messenger and stake my all on the wire-fed noises that come out of it in return. Not thinkable, not possible, it's a question of aesthetics.

Memory, then. Perception. Interpretation. Brain work – you're always on about your oh so superior and voluminous brain, go ahead and bloody use it. Think back on tonight. You looked at her, OK, with eyes that had no shutters on? You yanked up your jalousie and flashed your soul? How did she respond? That glow, that flicker – was it merely the reflection of the torches that Masetto had placed there as footlighting, or was it a flame that you yourself had kindled?

Silence? Surely you know the answer to that, Henry, don't you? You don't? You surprise me. No, worse, you disappoint me. You can't fool me, I know perfectly well what it is. You don't know because you don't want to know. You don't *dare* to know, in case . . . See, you haven't even got the guts to let me finish. Well, cling to your doubts then, you craven old clown, and cling to your hopes, and cling to your bottle, and flop yourself down on the hammock so that you can dangle there all night in this limbo, seeing you're so scared of leaving it. Swing, swing, that's it. Rock a bye baby. Eeny meeny miney mo. She loves me, she loves me not. Keep swaying, Henry, you're a pain in the rectum. *Buona notte, liebe Lotte.*

*ORSO MARIA – SERENADE TO A MOBILE PHONE

Littlest. My little seal pup. Where are you? On the beach? Yes, I expect you're basking on the beach. Lucky you. Look, my precious, something has cropped up, something to do with the case – too long to explain but unfortunately it means I can't make it Saturday. You deserve someone much younger, you know. You should never have got involved with a busy old wretch like me. Why don't you stay on by the sea for another few days, eh? Not to worry about expenses – that's my province – that's all I'm good for. Oh, and don't try to ring me: my phone will be off, I'm afraid. All these meetings, you know . . . Be in touch, be in touch.

ISOBEL – RECITATIVE
WITH A BIRO

Louise J. Shapiro, M.D.
57 Brattle Street, Cambridge, Massachusetts – 02138
– USA
August 8th '99

Dearest Lula,
It's back to the Middle Ages here, but then, you will
say, isn't that what we came all this way to find. A
couple of nights back we had a summer storm and the
house took a direct hit: now phone is not working,
icebox is off, pool is stagnant and sprouting algae,
computer has snapped it completely, and Milton's
television is literally sky, having blown up and disin-
tegrated into the Umbrian air. Amen.

Technicians have come from far and wide and
fiddled around and whipped out their pocket calcu-
lators – which work just fine, wouldn't you know –
and assure us it's only a question of re-wiring the entire
place at a cost of x dollars, where x is a way over the
five thousand mark. But Milton has gone all paranoid
and says he won't pay up, that they're a gang of
leeches and Italy is rotten all through and how right
his grandfather was to get the hell out when he did,
and now he's trying to fix things himself with the aid
of local talent – a guy we met on the set of this opera

affair we're both taking part in and who we hope is a better electrician than actor. So far however . . . well, you can judge yourself from the ballpoint.

Robert Klein flies back tomorrow morning and will mail this for me from the airport when he gets in, so I reckon, unless he forgets, it's my fastest way of reaching you. No, don't bring good coffee, I've still got plenty. Yes, do bring sun-block, the stuff here is untrustworthy, 16 is the highest factor you can get, and we've bought up the last stock. No one in Italy seems to have heard of skin cancer. That's local colour for you – basal-cell brown.

You say our summer activities sound anachronistic. Well, so they do, maybe, but wait till you see us on the night. Plenty of Earls and Dukes in showbusiness on our side of the Atlantic too – doesn't necessarily mean they don't know their job. You want to be a little more democratic, Lula, in your approach. OK, Lord Thirsk is a dilettante and a misogynist and looks like he came out of the giraffe pen of the zoo, and personally I have a very, very fraught relationship with him indeed, but as a director he has his qualities. (Not to mention when he takes to the stage himself in the role of the Commendatore – talk about being made of stone!) Milton is miscast, you say. Milton is not miscast: Milton has great stage dignity, ideal for the part of Octavio, and it was only thanks to Lord Thirsk's intuition that this quality came to the fore. If you've heard comments to the contrary it is because people are envious, and because, on the brink of the millennium though we are, titles are still titles, and a British Lord is still a

British Lord, and there are dozens of neighbours of ours who carp and carp and inside are just slavering to be part of the show, so there. This little old English bit-part actor guy plays Leporello, told me he's been receiving hate mail ever since he accepted the part. Hate mail, as in Hollywood or somewhere. Mind you, he could have been joking – Londoners have a weird sense of humour. But even so, that's the atmosphere: pretty electric.

Yeah, yeah, spare the wisecrack, it'll be working all right by the time you show up, if not we'll all move out into a hotel, promise. Not such a bad idea either, power or no power: I may tell you, we've had a few *arrière pensées* lately about our choice of summer residence. However, Lord Thirsk – Henry as I call him now – has certainly livened things up as regards this season. Can't wait for you to train your clinical analyst's eye on him. Not homosexual, no, that's partly where his relationships with the opposite sex flounder; my guess would be more that he was gravely abused by some adult female figure when a kid – flagellated, perhaps, by a corseted English nurse on the ramparts of the family castle. Oh oh. Anyway he clearly cannot deal with brains or personality in a woman – witness the winsome little wife, all curves and submission, and the way during yesterday's re-hearsal he just *gloried* in handing my part to an understudy who checks out round about six foot, while I stood by and watched her make a hash of it. OK I had a throat problem, but all the same I could see it was done to provoke a response from yours truly. (And he'll get one all right when my vocal cords start re-vibrating. You know your Bel when she is roused.)

One quick piece of advice before I close: take a numbered cab from *outside* of the airport building – one of those yellow or white ones that have a proper display meter. The drivers that sidle up to you *inside* the building whispering, *Taxi* like it was hashish or something are sharks. Sorry we can't make it to pick you up in person, but our hired car is – yes, you've got it – kaput, to kaput it mildly.

See you Tuesday. Come bring us cheer and sun-block and a whiff of civilisation along with your own sweet self,

Isobel

JOURNALIST –
RECITATIVE IN PRINT

Assoc. 'Friends of Foligno' – Monthly Newsletter.
August '99

Southumbria Hits Back

Exactly a year after Peter Brook stages his spare, thought-provoking production of Mozart's *Don Giovanni* for the Aix-en-Provence Festival, one meridian further south, in what the tourist brochures call the Green Heartland of Italy, another team gets to grips with the same time-honoured theme. Rivalry? An Anglo-Italian gauntlet thrown in the face of the transalpine cousins? Or could it be homage, or simple coincidence?

Before attempting an answer, let's take a look at the plucky company who are presently working on the project. First the director himself: aristo, author, historian and all round littérateur, Lord Henry Thirsk. Lord Henry, when I run him to ground on the set during a rehearsal, admits candidly to a dilettante approach. 'Never staged an opera before,' he tells me in his plummy Old-Etonian drawl. 'Enormous fun to try. Great challenge.' He widens his silk shirtsleeves in a gesture that includes all those present. 'I'd like to take this opportunity to say how terrifically lucky I have been in my collaborators.'

Gracious words, or the truth? Aix was able to engage the

conducting skills of an Abbado. Who is looking after the musical side of this more homespun production? And who are the singers?

Lord Henry chuckles engagingly. 'Oh, the tops,' he says, 'the very tops,' but declines to reveal any further information. On stage I espy Lord Henry's vivacious young Italian wife, Gaia, their niece Emily, over on an extended visit, and a neighbour of theirs, the well-known antique dealer and man-about-country, Francesco Pianese. Donna Elvira, Zerlina and Don Giovanni, respectively. All appear to be carrying small, suspicious-looking pocket tape recorders. Could it be this glittering amateur cast is actually cheating and using playback?

Thirsk gives another mischievous chuckle when I quiz him on this point and lays a finger on his droopy upper-class lip, but rebuts accusations of nepotism and chauvinism. 'We're a mixed bag,' he insists. 'Two Americans,' and he points to his other leading lady, the striking Mrs Marcucci and economist husband Milton, who fill the roles of Donna Anna and Ottavio – companions on stage as in everyday life. 'Three Italians.' And here, alongside Elvira and Don Giovanni, he indicates peasant hero, Masetto, played by the versatile young local electrician, Federico Baciucco, also in charge of lighting effects. 'Not to mention,' with a deprecating prod at his own breastbone, 'our English trio, namely: self, my niece Emily who you've already met, and our star turn and only professional element, the well-known comic actor Wilfred Fletcher.'

Fletcher (best remembered as a Keatonesque dead-pan Bottom in the '85 Birmingham Fringe production of *A Midsummer Night's Dream*) is nowhere to be found.

'Doesn't willingly talk to press before a show,' Lord Henry explains. 'Artistic temperament, you know.'

Nodding understandingly, I go on to enquire about scenery and costumes, of which there is as yet little trace in the austere Montaldo *piazza* where the opera is due to be staged in only ten days' time. Is this deliberate? A minimalist approach on the part of designers Volpi and Rossi d'Avola? Or are they too, like comic star Fletcher/Leporello, banking on the surprise factor?

D'Avola ('Drop the Contessa, please, it sounds so unprofessional') laughingly denies any attempt at secrecy. Costumes are nearly ready, she says, and, no, they can in no way be described as minimalist or untraditional; she has gone overboard to make them simply as pretty and eye-catching as she possibly can. When taxed about rumours of discord between her and scenographer Volpi, she dismisses them as unfounded. 'On the contrary,' she says, 'we've liaised perfectly from the start.'

Volpi, rangy, blonde-haired artist wife of the prominent Roman lawyer, corroborates. Linking arms, the pair mount the as yet unfurbished stage where they pose among wood-shavings and carpenter's clutter for the photographer of the *Todi Gazette*. Media coverage is not a problem, their confident faces seem to say. With this sort of talent and this sort of team spirit, who could disagree? Umbria may have to bow to Provence's superior resources and experience, but director Thirsk and his jet-set *équipe* look poised to provide local audiences with a night to remember.

(Pro memoria for the indomitable: Venue: Montaldo, piazza della Libertà. Sole performance: Tuesday 24th August, 9.30 p.m. Seats – unnumbered and uncushioned –

10,000 lire; free admission for children under twelve. Profits go towards a new changing room for Montaldo Football Club who lost their old one through earthquake damage, so at least it's all in a good cause. What else can be said? *Forza* Montaldo! Looks as if you'll need it.)

AMABILE – ARIA

The Avvocato was here this afternoon. Right here in this house, sitting on this sofa. On top of all the comics – he turned up so unexpectedly I didn't have time to tidy, just to shove them under the cushions and hope he didn't notice. He's not a man for visits as a rule – it's not that he gives himself airs, it's just that he's far too busy. You see him on television sometimes, hurrying out of places with his robes flapping and all the journalists following. Doesn't even stop for the cameras. And he's often in the papers: Beppe saw a photograph only last month.

And yet today he was here, sitting and talking as if time was no problem, drinking coffee like a friend. He's taken over the whole business to do with Lucia, says his firm will deal with everything, and we're not to worry about expenses. We'll come to some arrangement later, he said, Beppe can put in extra hours in the garden or something, we'll work it out between ourselves. He didn't promise he'd get her off, or even sound all that hopeful it could be done, but he was so calm and capable that I nearly cried, the relief was so great. After that I hardly liked to remind him of the other help he'd promised – over the insurance, I mean, and the difficulty we're having collecting – but then I thought to myself, if we have the money we could at least get him a nice present when it's all over and show our thanks that way, and anyway, it's either now or never, and we've troubled him so much already that a little more bother can hardly hurt . . .

He was good about that too. Said how sorry he was he'd forgotten. Just leave it to me, Amabile, he said, I'll get your money out of these vultures for you, in record time, down to the last lira. And if you really want to do something in return to thank me, then I'd appreciate it if you kept quiet about this visit with my wife. That's all I ask. Things aren't going too well between us at the moment, as you may have noticed, and I don't want her to go thinking that with this gesture of mine I'm trying to worm my way back into her graces. Nor do I want you and Beppe to go thinking it either. This is a private matter, OK, between the three of us?

Whatever he's been up to these weeks in Rome, I call that real gentlemanly behaviour. And to do him justice I must say that Giovanna *is* a bit careless about him sometimes – leaving him all that freedom. A man like him, with that car and those looks and that place in the world – in a way it's asking for trouble. Sometimes she's careless about his clothes too, and he's such a one for being nicely groomed. An Italian wife would fuss over him more and keep him on a shorter lead, and I'm not sure she wouldn't do right. As I've said before, men around a certain age can get themselves into such bothers: the head seems to go soft while other bits I could name don't.

He knows his job though, you can say that for him, brain's sharp enough there. I feel much more comfortable now he's taken the reins. Knows all the right people too. He seems to think, seeing as Lucia didn't have anything else on her other than the drugs – no lists of contacts or

146

telephone numbers or address books or whatever it is they go looking for in these cases – he seems to think it's possible the judge in charge may do a deal: get the police to drop charges in exchange for her agreeing to go into one of these centres where they break the habit. There's one run by priests just the other side of Perugia, which'd be ideal, as Beppe and I could pop over there weekends and take her the things she needs, but I told the Avvocato distance was no problem and if only we could get her in – anywhere – I'd crawl to Milan and back on my knees.

He kissed me when he left. What a kind man, and he does smell nice. Now all I've got to do is wait and hope. Oh, yes, and hold my tongue with Giovanna, which will be more difficult than the other two things put together. I wish I'd never made that promise now, because I know it's the first thing I'll want to do tomorrow morning: tell her what a good man she's married to, all things considered, and to forget and forgive, and take him back, and stop chattering on the telephone to that other man, whoever he is, who's always ringing. The foreign one. Don't worry, Amabile, she says, it's only about the scenery for the opera; he's got a wife and a very pretty one too – half my age. Well, if that's so, why doesn't he talk to his wife, then? I'm sure Beppe doesn't spend half his morning on the phone with another woman, and if he did, and I caught him at it, he wouldn't hear the end of it. Foreigners are different, so they say, but not this one. Oh, no, I'm no fool, I know what this one's made like, *and* I know what he's after. I can hear it in the voice – that eagerness, that mealy, tomcat-on-the-tiles purr. *C'è la*

Signora, prrrego? Not for you, I'd like to tell him. You stay away from her, she's got problems enough with men as it is.

It's strange, with all that's been going on I haven't had time to go down to Stefano and water the plants and change the water in the vases, but instead of fretting, I've begun to feel it doesn't matter. He's here inside me really, closer than ever, and a few wilted flowers on the headstone aren't going to alter that. Or are they? Look after the living, Mammà, I fancy I can hear him say. Save your legs and look after Lucia and the boys, and then when the worry is over, if you *must*, you can bring me a cactus that won't need so much tending. Is this a good sign, I wonder, or a bad? I used to despise people who couldn't go to the bother of fresh flowers for their loved ones' graves. Does it mean I'm getting over his death or just getting used to it? I don't know, and I don't know which is better or which is worse; all I know is I've lost him once through someone else's fault and I don't want to lose him now through mine.

But life drags you on, doesn't it? And better thirsty flowers than thirsty animals, if you have to choose, and it's not as if a cactus was a plastic plant . . . Anyway we'll see. Those flowering varieties are beautiful, some of them, and when the insurance money comes in – as I'm sure it will do soon, now the Avvocato's taken charge – I could splash out on a big bronze vase to keep the pot in. There's a lovely one on display in that shop on the road to Deruta, shape of an angel. I wouldn't feel so bad somehow, leaving my Steffi with an angel.

Silly old softie, I can hear him say – he always used to

laugh at my fancies: angel or weasel or just plain vase, what difference does it make?

I don't know, my treasure, forgive your silly old mother who never had much schooling, but it does.

JOANNA – ARIA

So busy this week painting and finishing the sets, I haven't had time to file my nails but have had to shorten them in bed at night by dint of chewing. (Even them up, that is: several I have broken already, scrabbling away at the other sort.) I have a terrible cramped way of holding my paint-brushes, and actually wound myself if the fingernails get too long. Toes I can ignore in summer, thanks to sandals, otherwise I'd have probably had to do the same job on them as well, if I could still reach them.

What would Orso say? He is so finicky about things like that, he'd have a fit. But Orso says nothing because Orso is not here.

Advantages of solitude:
Nail-chewing ad lib.
Meals when you like, of food that you like.
Free work-schedule.
No telly blaring, except for news.
No flutters inside: what the eye doesn't see, the heart still grieves over maybe, but the stomach doesn't lurch over. Or even twitch over.

Little else. The bed gets hot in summer, but I still occa-sionally miss the animal presence of my faithless old mate at my side, in my lair. Habit, I suppose. (And even this is dwindling: in fact, after his failure to help out over the Lucia business, I'm not sure it isn't broken altogether. Nails again – the last in the coffin of my love.)

As to his whereabouts I have no idea, and strangely enough very little curiosity either. The telephone – most annoyingly with all this work – has taken to ringing and then going abruptly silent when answered. Experience, and a kind of related sensibility that I've developed to radar pitch over the years, tells me it's the current flame; and experience, coupled with reason in this case, also tells me that things are breaking up on that front. She doesn't know where he is either; he's stopped informing her about his movements. Ah. Poor kid, her hold on him is slipping. But what the hell – she should never have taken him on without references, and I could have given her plenty of those.

I could have sent her the score of *Don Giovanni* for a start. It's all there: the restlessness, the yearning, the ageing male fleeing from the twilight, from the grave, from the fast accumulating proof of the waning of his powers. Where can he run? Towards a bright mirror, held for him by some accommodating nymph, that is where. Look here, old wanderer. Take a dekko in my glass. See how fetching you still are. But the snag is that the mirror, to catch the light, must be held against the sun, so that in reality with every step he takes he hastens further and further into the night, getting tireder and tireder and less and less fetching as he goes. The spectator knows this, and the fugitive knows it too, but once the flight is on, it becomes more and more difficult for him to accept this fact and to turn round and trudge back in the proper direction.

I have a male side too – witness the size of my feet. Perhaps, like people say, artists are all a bit androgynous.

And this side of me understands and sympathises, and even gives a half-hearted cheer. I think of Dylan Thomas urging his father to go out raging, and I whisper secretly to Orso, low, so the other side of me won't hear: Very well, old comrade of mine, if raging for you means screwing, then go out screwing, you have my blessing. It'd have been nice if we could have stood and fought the enemy together, but there it is: *Titanic* time, every man for himself.

Only the other side does hear, of course, she hears everything, and she tells me I'm a wimp and a traitor. Every *man*, she says. Exactly: the women bustle round with blankets and hot cocoa, and the men scarper with the sirens. You make me sick, Joanna. Talk about Elvira – you're far worse. How many years is it now that you've traipsed along behind your Don Giovanni, holding up his real image and begging him to look at it, instead of the fake one? 'OK, you're getting on a bit, and your hair's thinning and your waist isn't, and you're a swindler and a rake and a coward, but there's still someone who likes you that way, who still sees the good parts.' How many times have you taken him back when the rival mirror cracked and delusion set in? How many times have you believed him when he said this was the last? Ten? Twelve? More? Or don't you like to count?

I'll tell you what, she says, you should have married someone like Henry, that's what. Henry is another kettle of fish. Henry is *company*. Henry is one of those rare males who would have been among the cocoa servers. Better still, he'd have been in the orchestra, playing lovely tunes to you to keep your spirits up. His mind is stocked chock-a-block with goodies that'll last. Sex appeal? Physical allure?

Animal presence in the bed? In the second half of the life match who cares about perishable commodities such as those? No, you should have had more foresight and bagged yourself a Henry. What do you mean, it's too late now? It isn't, and you know it. Do something for me, will you, please? No, no, I'm not asking for anything committing, like smiling at him in a meaningful way or letting a little note of availability creep into your voice when you talk to him – nothing like that; I'm merely asking you to let your mind dwell on him – in a purely, *purely* hypothetical way, you understand – as a . . . No, don't be so hasty, not even as a suitor, just as a stand-in, as a place-marker for some putative candidate in the future who may or may not show up. Think about him a little. Or someone like him. Imagine to yourself life at his side, or – very well – at the side of someone not so different. And then see if, slowly, slowly the picture doesn't begin to grow on you.

What was that? *Disloyalty*? For Christ's sake, woman! At this point you'd be entitled to grind your way through a platoon of Henrys in the flesh before disloyalty caught up with you, and all I'm asking is that you take *one*, in *spirit*, and just hold him in your head in a speculative way to see if . . . Nothing, just to see. You will? Good. (Whew! That took some doing.)

Mmm. A Henry, she says. A Henry look-alike or a Henry talk-alike? A Henry both of course, since they almost invariably go together. And there lies the problem. I tried an experiment the other night, to see into myself as deep as I could on these matters. I imagined myself in an end-of-the-world situation: an archipelago composed of three little islands, and the human population reduced to three entities, myself, a blond Bay Watch hunk of manhood, and an ageing philosopher of the Bertrand Russell cast, each of us stranded on a different island. The others have no transport but I have a leaky boat that can only be used the once. Towards which island do I set sail? Shame on me (because his lifesaving skills don't come into it in the slightest), but I go hunkwards every time.

What does this mean? I'm not sure I really want to spell it out to myself, but in practical terms I think it means that as regards future male companionship I am condemned to solitude. Hunks are off the menu, and with tastes like that I don't deserve a soul mate, even if one were available. As that little song by Mozart goes I love so much: *Buona notte, liebe Lotte, Bonne nuit, gute Nacht, good-night.*

And now back to work. Bossy Flossie has delivered the costumes to Henry and he has promised to bring them over tomorrow evening. (Or was it this evening? No, no, tomorrow, I'm sure he said tomorrow.) That'll be more on my plate still. Although with glue and razor and good lick of shoe blacking, shouldn't take long . . .

LOUISE – RECITATIVE
TO TAPE RECORDER

Martin, this is me – yeah, well, I've caught this throat thing that's going around – talking to you from beside a bright-green swimming pool somewhere in the heart of Central Italy. I mean the centre of the heartland of – oh, leave it. I'm with the Marcuccis – Bel and Milton. Their number is on that little red pad on my work desk. Martin, this is a mayday message. I can't speak over the phone because there's always someone around and it sounds so discourteous to whisper when you're a guest, and I can't reach a callbox either as the nearest one is five vertical miles away, but I need rescuing. Do something for your poor stranded mom. Something effective, but at the same time diplomatic – something that's not going to scare me too much, or upset my hosts, but that's going to get me right out of here faster than a . . . can't think of anything fast enough . . . than a snake or whatever. (Snakes are a bit on my mind at present, I'll explain later. So are mice: I reckon it's the candle grease attracts them. So are flies, so are spiders, so are frogs – the pool's full of them. So are earthquakes.) What should you do? Well, you're the one goes to MIT. Think up something and then do it quick. A cable – something about Grandma Bayliss – about a patient of mine – I don't know. Just as long as it works. No, not cable: deliveries don't seem to be too punctual. Make it a call and make it fast. And whatever you do, keep ringing: the line's a bit . . .

Whirr.

What's happened to this thing? Is it the battery? Christ Almighty, the tape's coming out like pasta out of the machine. How the fuck's sake can I send . . .

Click.

HENRY – ARIA

What is love? countered Jesus, jest for jest, and wouldn't stay for an answer either. Well, and what is it? Who is this madcap *condottiere* who has taken over the poor, ill-drilled troops of my brain, whirling them away behind his standard? Their old leaders, Prudence, Judgement, Reason, tag along behind and bleat out counter-orders, but too late and in vain: the momentum is up, the wild sortie goes ahead.

Everything I do, every breath I take, every footling little action I perform, is dusted over with a magic powder. I call up the electrician and the mere fact that he has spent half the morning with Joanna and mentions her name to me makes me half fall in love with him too. What a nice man, I think, what a nice conversation we are having. All of a sudden I remember his cousin, who used to drive for us before, and words of sympathy that I usually find so hard to utter come flowing out of my mouth, smoother than out of the Duchess of Kent's at Ladies' Finals. I congratulate him on his performance as Masetto also while I am about it. He demurs, pleased; warms towards me; for a split second we are in contact on a plane other than the mundane one on which we normally meet. *Bravo, Masetto, sta' mi bene.* Take care with all those wires, won't you. I make other calls, leaving behind me a little touch of Henry wherever I alight. I may not be a memorable Commendatore but I think I am, in my small-town way, a bloody *inspired* director. Sensitivity, flair, authority, intimate knowledge of the score – all I was lacking was what la Marcwhatsit calls 'relational skills', and now abracadabra and I have those too.

With Flossie Rossi I need them, and how. She nails me to the blower for a good quarter of an hour with a tirade that almost burns my ear off, but since it is all about Joanna, and Joanna's atrocious scenery and atrocious taste and atrocious character and atrocious manners, I enjoy myself no end. As it is with publicity, it is the space that counts: no matter in what key or context, I can talk about her, think about her, say her name over and over in a crescendo of zest till I nearly pop. Yes, Florence, you've said it, she is a weirdo. No, not butch, I don't think, but yes, those clothes of hers are a bit draggy. Yeah, yeah, no wonder the husband goes off after other women; can't be much fun having to make love all the time to a female paratrooper, quite. (Can't it? *Can't* it?) Interfering? Overbearing? Sabotaging your contribution? Surely not, Florenza, dear. Although . . . yeah, yeah, yeah, I agree . . . Marxist? We – ell, subversive's more like it, wouldn't you say? Absolutely. Couldn't agree more. Uhuh, uhuh. That's right, ignore her, you just go ahead and do your thing and let her do hers. Bruce Willis in a tutu? Ah, I see what you mean, a clash of styles, but not to worry, on the night it'll all blend beautifully. Relax, Flo, relax, that side of things is my responsibility. You just hand over the stuff and . . . Hangers? Plastic covers? Someone to do last-minute ironing and alterations? Yes, I think you'll find all that will be laid on OK, you know how good our local ladies are with their needles. What? Sorry, I thought you said meretricious. Oh, the costumes – delicious. Mmmn, I'm sure they are. Barry Lyndon? Yes, I did. Les Liaisons Dangereuses too. Wonderful, Florence. Clever you. No, I won't let We-Know-Who get her grubby paws on them until I have to, and, yes, send me the bill from Harrods, that's my responsibility too. Goodness. Wow. Wouldn't you have done better to stick to Foligno? No, no, not a criticism, just an observation. Ah, to counteract the shabbiness of . . . I see. No, how right you are, she has no class, no class at all.

True and splendid and amazing. She has no class, my beloved, she fits in no pre-established category, she is unclassifiable, unique. Logicians would correct me and say she belongs to a class which contains only one member: herself. But what do logicians know about such things? I long for her, I thirst for her, the time I spend without her is condemned time: I can't do anything with it except kill it. Whack! over the head like my clement old mum used to do with practically every living thing she encountered. Put it out of its misery, put it out of its misery.

One consolation I cling to: whatever happens, whichever way the threads of our destinies unroll, whether entwined or separate or tangled in an unholy mess, this span of scorching Umbrian summer is the high point of my life. An old record from my childhood spins through my head, cracks and static and all, unleashing the strains of a cosmopolitan voice that sounds as if it must have sounded foreign in every language it spoke. Sacha Guitry, could it be? *These ees my luffly day, Thees ees the day I will remember the day I'm dying. They can't take thees away, Eet will be always mine, the sun and the wine, the seagulls flying . . .*

Swifts for me here inland, not seagulls, and mercifully a whole season (and perhaps longer still if my luck holds), but I subscribe humbly to the entire text. Another Henry in another mood would have turned aside fastidiously, muttering some caustic comment about corn and chaff, but to glowing old Henry, mellowed by love, the words seem impossible to improve on. This is indeed my *aestas aurea*, my golden summer. Mozart's *Don Giovanni* has always been my favourite work of art, stealing the prize from every other artistic creation, be it music or poem or play or film or painting, but now it is more to me still: it is the casket in which this golden treasure is enclosed. As I say, I have no idea what the future has in store for myself and Joanna as a joint entity, if anything at all, but from now onwards I will only have to open the score of the opera, or post one of my many CD versions into my machine, for the memory of her to come surfing back to me on the notes. Mine. In this dimension, always mine. Nay, should we never meet to sense, our souls would hold intelligence.

Tonight I went to see her, to deliver the costumes. She wasn't there when I arrived. Out bestowing her presence on some luckier friend: afraid I must have misunderstood her over the telephone, or given her the wrong day. So I mooched around her domain like a fetishist, inhaling her traces and getting high on them. Her clothes, her cigarette butts, the music she'd been listening to, a pile of walnut husks she'd been cracking with a hammer – I lingered over them all, trying to add to my pitifully small knowledge of who she really is and how she lives. Part of me pitied myself on opposite grounds: closer than this, you old fool, it told me, you will never come, and if you do, you'll only regret it.

Sniff away and snoop away, and then sneak away if you are wise.

This counsel I ignored: it was Henry the Humble speaking and I'll say it again *fortissimo*, he's a spasm in the sigmoid.

The answerphone was blinking: I longed to poach her messages, in order to see what the vile Volpi is up to – I don't know why but I have a kind of skin sensation, eczema or worse, that he is here, somewhere in the offing, contemplating a recuperative manoeuvre before it's too late. I think I've seen that flashy car of his crawling round the neighbourhood recently, up to no good. But I didn't dare. Instead I went into the studio, and there I received a surprise, which I'm not quite sure whether to classify as positive or negative, since on the one hand it makes the winning of her more improbable still, and on the other fills me with straightforward joy on her account. Joanna can paint. If she wants to she really can paint.

There was an easel in one corner of the studio, and on it a half-finished painting of a woman, sitting on a terrace on a cane chair in the sunlight. An ordinary painting by Joanna's standards, at first sight an ordinary woman. Then, as you stand looking at her, the spell which every work of art, great or small, possesses by definition, begins to work, and things that it shouldn't be possible to reproduce anyhow, let alone by the slender means of pigment and canvas, start wafting out at you. Purity, for example; suffering, courage, forbearance, generosity, all sorts of all too rare human qualities. And all sorts of atmospheric qualities too: the warmth of the day, the vibrant stillness of the air – bees perhaps in the background, the scent of lavender, the growl of a far-off tractor. I don't know who the woman is – if indeed she is any one particular individual and not just an emblem for an entire species – and I'm perfectly aware that if I met her I wouldn't be able to get through to her at all: huge hedges of class and gender and education would stand between us, obscuring the view both ways. But translated here for me by Joanna I can pierce the very core of her, puncture the lining of her soul, feel something for her akin to brotherly love, if that doesn't sound too mawkish.

With this gift, why for the sake of Crippen does Joanna spend her artistic energies on the manure heaps? Contemporary art is such a conundrum to me. I see of course that a small portion of it, when seriously produced (which I hold to be very rarely indeed), is intended to convey what you might call a meta-artistic message to the receiver. A message *about* art, that is, couched for convenience in a pseudo-artistic idiom: either to tell you that art is dead, slain by the bourgeois equation Value = Money, or else that if it isn't dead yet it should be, or else that the artist simply finds the framework it presently offers too fettering for work purposes and is therefore trying to enlarge it at your expense – something like that. Joyce did it for literature, after all: bent the cage, broke the tools, invented new ones. (And most people would agree, no, that his books have served some purpose beyond, like mine, the propping of rickety bedsteads?) This sort of argument – though it might be less confusing if carried on in another medium, in the newspapers, say, or over the blooming Internet – I can accept as valid. The guy, or the doll, is after all trying to *tell* you something, however much you may disagree with it or wish it untold. What I *cannot* accept is the consequence this waiving of the rules has led to: this horde of non-serious, untalented, unscrupulous con-artists and con-connoisseurs, flooding the art markets with their tawdry wares that no one dares expose for what they are, namely bilge and tripe and bollocks.

It is obscene that an artefact – by anyone, even Leonardo or Phidias, let alone that demented visionary of a Van Gogh – should cost a quarter of a hundred million quid. The price does not reflect the esteem in which art is held in our society, merely our greed. I heard over the news some while back that a schoolboy on a museum visit had stuck a pencil through a Matisse, causing uproar among art lovers the world over. To my mind the child should have received, not a prize, naturally, since picture-sticking is not a pastime to be encouraged any more than people-sticking or animal-sticking or anything-sticking, but a simple reprimand from his teacher and maybe a fine to cover the canvas repair. That would have put both the transgression *and* the Matisse in their proper perspectives. 'That'll be 95p, you little sod, and next time we'll take you to the Fontana exhibition and let you do your damnedest.' (For the man who took the hammer to Michelangelo's Madonna, on the other hand . . . ah, well, man is contradictory by nature . . . I would have upped the price and made him pay congruously through the nose.)

All these things I look forward to discussing with Joanna some day. If I have not yet done so it's because I too have a craven streak. It's not so much that I am afraid of hurting her – although that comes into it too: it's more that I am terrified, with such fogeyman opinions, of seeming old. Gaia accepts my fifty-seven-year-old chassis with its far earlier dated motor, but I'm not sure Joanna either would or could. Paradoxical, when of the two Gaia is a full decade younger, but there it is.

HENRY AND JOANNA – DUET

HENRY: It was so late when Joanna finally got back that I was already in my car with the engine running, on the point of leaving. She asked me in for a drink, but the house is badly lit externally and – stupid, boss-eyed fool that I am – I thought I detected politeness on her face where there should have been something quite different and said a rather stiff and chippy no before I stopped myself. Not me at all, but since when have I been me? Then I turned on the headlights and could have bitten out my tongue: there was a look in her eyes I had never seen before, not off stage at any rate, and not aimed in my direction – a wistful, soft, entreating look. A look teeming with unsaid meanings and untapped possibilities. Wait, Henry. Stay, Henry. Say nothing, do nothing, but don't for God's sake go away, not now, not yet . . .

JOANNA: That's it. I've blown it, whatever it was or might have been. Awful, my forgetting like that: I'm sure he said tomorrow, but I suppose before accepting Claudia's invitation to dinner I should have rung up and checked. Perhaps it's a good thing I didn't, though. When I came through the gate and saw him waiting there in the car I had such a rush of pleasure . . . I can't explain it, I felt about eighteen. I felt cherished, female, and oh, so tempted to . . .

HENRY: If she had seen that I had seen, I think that might have been it. I would most probably and most willingly have stalled the car and tumbled out into the night and on to the gravel and lain there at her feet. Henry the landed haddock, to be done with as she wished. But she hadn't seen that I'd seen, she couldn't have, so my blasted cowardice or reserve or rectitude or whatever it is retained the upper hand, and I chugged past her, burning inside with hope and passion but outwardly unconsumed and stolid as a Christmas pudding under the brandy flames. See you tomorrow. Yes, see you tomorrow. Don't work too hard. I won't.

JOANNA: To do what? Fall into his arms? Strip my clothes off and throw myself on the sofa and beckon? Unthinkable. Unfeasible. Marriage is terrible that way – it rusts up all your angling equipment. I am worse than a virgin, I can't even flirt any more. With Orso I must have made love – oh, what would it be, somewhere between two and three thousand times, and with each time I seem to have lost more and more of my general expertise at the expense of the particular. I know more and more about his needs, that is, and less and less about other men's.

HENRY: Oh, and . . . Yes? What? (Lurch, brake. Rev up again, false alarm.) Give my love to Gaia. Your love to Gaia? That not: your love, my love, if love it is or ever will be, I will keep for myself. All of it, down to the last little crumb. And tomorrow I will risk the high jump and give you mine. Take it or leave it – can't pussyfoot around on the run up any longer – must either soar or crash.

JOANNA: Although Henry, I must say, is not just another man. I think I realised that for the first time tonight – how special he is and how, yes, how engaging and, in his funny boffin way, attractive. Perhaps not sexually, exactly, but attractive the way gravity is: possessing some force, some invisible quantum that pulls me towards him. His laugh – that slightly equine snort with the thrown-back head. His diffidence. The silk shirt, the immaculately clean nails, the way he crosses his legs, one hoisted high over the other, and then taps at his ankle. Elegance, nonchalance, and other eighteenth-century qualities ending in 'nce' that I can't presently think of. Tolerance, maybe. Balance. What I think of as Whig virtues, don't quite know why. The sort of things I associate with my father. Not because he exhibited them himself – as a country solicitor he was much stuffier and staider – but because they were what he would have liked to exhibit if he'd dared. Refined is a burnt-out word, but if you think of it in a laboratory sense, or a cooking sense, then that is what Henry is: a filtrate of good, proven English ingredients. Like steak and kidney pie. And like steak and kidney pie he seems to typify for me our distinctive island blend of savagery and civilisation. Hooome, as ET whimpered when he was so far away from his: Hooome. An English man, an Englishman, Fee, fi, fo, fum.

HENRY: Tomorrow. Yes. Tomorrow. But when? And how? Tonight's occasion was so perfect it is unlikely to reoccur. And if I muffed it, the way I've just gone and done, doesn't this mean I'll muff the next? And the next and the next, because I simply don't and can't . . .? Oh piss off, Henry II, it's just . . . this fragile, gossamer happiness, I'm frightened of losing it or doing anything to place it in jeopardy. Better the rack than the block.

JOANNA: Absurd after I've known him properly for such a short time, but I felt devastated when he left. For a moment I thought he would read the message I was trying to send (that was about as far as I could get: goggle, the way I used to as a child at those of my father's friends who caught my fancy, scaring them to death). But he either didn't get it or didn't want to, and off he rolled down the drive and I felt the night close round me again with a scrunch, as if I was being wrapped up in paper, prior to being stowed away. In September I shall be forty-five.

HENRY: No, you idiot, the block was a privilege. (You should know that all right. I seem to remember you saying it apropos your erstwhile chauffeur in order to raise a queasy laugh among your dinner guests. Mr and Mrs Flage and their son Percy – great buddy of yours, that Percy Flage.) It was the rack you wanted to avoid. And still do. Better the block, therefore, better the block – especially with such a sweet executioner. So bring down your blade, Joanna, tomorrow that ever is I'll stick my scrawny neck out and you bring down your blade.

JOANNA: Good thing it went off like it did, good thing. Lord knows what might have happened if he'd stayed.

This last betrayal of Orso's has made me so unstable. It's strange what an effect it has over time, a partner's infidelity. Like a wound, at first you feel numbness, then pain to screaming point, then weakness, and then, as the wound begins to scar, a novel kind of strength, born of indifference. And it's this strength, I think, that causes the instability: while you're weak you can't move; the moment you're strong again you think of going. Away. Anywhere. With the first acceptable travelling companion who shows up. And Henry – why didn't I see this before? – is a good deal more than acceptable, he's downright desirable, and the journey with him would be such a holiday, such a treat, compared to this sentimental gauntlet that Orso makes me run.

HENRY: But in the meantime, as is cynically permitted by society to those under sentence of death, let me relish tonight, the stars, your nearness. So close still that, although the car takes me further and further in the opposite direction, I almost feel my thoughts can reach you, and vice versa. What are you doing now? Heaving a sigh of relief that you're rid of me? Or regretting that I've gone? Cockily, I suspect the last. Are you upstairs or downstairs? Getting ready for bed, or smoking a final cigarette, or working in your studio, or what? Again, I suspect the second alternative: you're downstairs, disinclined to sleep, and you're smoking and painting at the same time. I can see you at it. Don't smoke too much.

JOANNA: Anyway, *finito*. *Finito* before it even began. And yet I feel so restless, and the evening feels so *un*finished.

My lonely bed is repugnant to me. What I might do is this: go into the studio, put *Don Giovanni* on the CD player to keep the scenes fresh in my mind, and get to grips with the costumes. Jo the Ripper. Just the sort of work I need.

HENRY: My marriage bed is anathema to me – Gaia has rigged up a mosquito net, and to lie under it is to languish in a hot, oppressive prison. So I'll tell you what I'm going to do, if you're interested: I'm going to listen to a little music. *Don Giovanni* again, so that Gaia, when she hears, will construe my restlessness as work-connected. Enrico has last-minute nerves about the opera / is adding last-minute corrections to his stage directions / making a last-minute hash of his already mangled translation of the score.

JOANNA: *Che contrasto d'affetti in sen ti nasce.* You can say that again. Seems written for me this bit: I really am in a morass. I'd like to talk to Vicky, but I can't, it's not right to pile anxiety on her at this distance. And then, she's Orso's daughter, she loves him, she loves us both. No, it wouldn't be right. Oh, stuff this organza, it's as thick as rhinoceros hide. What if I got at it with a blow lamp?

HENRY: Whereas in reality Enrico is dreaming *adagio* his adulterous dreams. Life is so short, Joanna, so absurd, and I fear it's all we're offered: why shouldn't I spend it with you? This tail end of happiness, why shouldn't I grab it? Suffering is everywhere, the whole planet is a factory of pain – to one small favoured creature is given a chance of a lifetime: it seems sheer cosmic churlishness to decline. If there were a God, and I were he, looking down on me, I would be furious to see such wastage. 'Miserable little runt,' I would say. 'Whinge, whinge, and when you're offered a taste of paradise you turn up your nose at it, on the grounds that it would be wrong. I can't think who gave you this killjoy notion, certainly not me. Stay in your treadmill, then, it's all you deserve. Look at Don Giovanni, listen to his parting cry – *No, no, ch'io non mi pento*. You think I let him drop into hell for that? Wrong, I caught him up at the last minute in my arms: he enjoyed my world, and for that alone he was worth saving. Not to mention his coherence, still less his guts. I like people with guts, you may have noticed. Yes, Lord Henry Lily Liver, I like people with guts.'

Oh, nonexistent God of mine, help me out, I am in a quagmire. Sorry? What was that, do you mind repeating? Work? Writing? You think so? Very well, anything for a bit of enlightenment, even the nefarious Napier, but I think I'll shift that to tomorrow too, if you don't mind. Tonight is for casket opening.

* GAIA – ARIA

Such a lovely summer, this, after getting off to a baddish start. It was silly of me to be so snooty about the opera – of course it's quite wrong for this country audience, and of course the production is cheap and shoddy and Joanna Volpi's attempts at trendiness only worsen matters, but it's really coming together well now, I think, and it's done *wonders* for Henry's morale. Kept him so busy and amused it just isn't true. And it *is* Mozart after all, which gives the whole thing a certain cachet – it's not as if he were spending all his energies on a musical or something trashy like that.

I've got my balance back too: he's been so sweet to me lately that he's sort of righted me, set me squarely on my feet again. I'd had a half-formed plan at the start of the season, that I didn't really like to confess to myself, it was so shaming, of sort of managing somehow to forget to take the pill, or anyway to skip one or two nights, to see if I couldn't get pregnant and keep my hold on him that way. I do so long for a child. But now I know that, precisely because I long for one, and because being a mother would be so important to me, I can't set a thing like that in motion with a trick. It wouldn't be fair to any of us – not to Henry, or the child, or even to me. If it happens, it's got to happen with all our blessings.

And now I've come to that decision, I feel kinder towards Emily, and easier in her company. It must have been jealousy that made me so ratty. I couldn't help looking

175

at her growing bigger and sleeker and prettier every day, and listening to her grumble about how hellish she feels, and watching her knock back the wine and light up cigarettes, and thinking how unfair it was she should be the one to be carrying a baby, not me. I wouldn't smoke, I wouldn't even want to. Nor would I throw myself into the pool like that – plash – face down in a belly flop on to the lilo: every time she does it I fear for a miscarriage. I don't know that I'd even give in to Henry's whim and leap around the stage as Zerlina – that dance he makes her do is pretty energetic, not to mention the seduction scene on the rubbish heap.

Ah well, I'm content at the moment just being me. Our première (silly word for it, but it *is* after all the first performance even if it's the last as well) is drawing near. Florence hasn't allowed us to see our finished costumes yet, but she tells me mine is ravishing. I've got half a mind to call in on Joanna, who's got them now, and take a peep. I love the clothes of that period: if I had a choice I'd like to have been born in Venice, the way I was, but a few centuries earlier. Lots of drawbacks, of course, and one would have *had* to have been in the right milieu – but, oh, those silks and velvets and flounces . . . mouth-watering.

Only blot on the day: a simply foul article came through the post in the 'Friends of Foligno' newsletter, which is read by every foreigner hereabouts and as far north as Chianti-shire. A send-up of Henry and the opera and all of us. Wilfred Fletcher was going to try through his agent to contact David Bowie, who lives somewhere over near Lake Trasimeno, and see if he couldn't persuade him to come and add some real glamour to the show, but now of course he won't want anything to do with us. Nobody will. How can people be so mean? Envy, I suppose. I wonder who wrote it? I shall have to try and find out. Although in a way I hardly want to, as it will mean making an enemy, and I am so bad at having enemies. I know it's childish and unrealistic but I like everyone to like me.

Just as I like liking everyone myself. Beware of the painter woman, Misa said last night over the phone, she sounds really bad news: unhappy wives are not to be trusted, they're always on the lookout for shoulders to cry on. Male shoulders, she added, well padded with banknotes. If you've got any sense you'll give her a good whack on her flabby old fanny and tell her to keep her distance. What do you mean, he's gone over to see her now? Isn't it evening with you? You must be out of your mind? Go and get the car, you idiot, and join them straightaway.

A few weeks ago this might have rattled me – although never enough to set me on the road: I'm very anti the sheepdog tactics that Misa and Mammà seem to think work so well with errant husbands – but not any more. We're friends now, me and Joanna, we really are. Until just recently I found her a bit off-putting quite honestly, because there was nothing I could seem to find to talk to her about. You know how you can usually get through to another woman on the subject of hair or clothes or slimming or servant problems – well, with her it was like trying to sew a piece of leather with a blunt needle. Stab, jab, and no further. Giggles about local hairdressers and the way they fluff you up like the *Roi Soleil* – no good because she doesn't go to hairdressers, local or otherwise (*and* you can see it). Fashion – same applies, you'd get more sense on the subject out of Emi, which is saying something. Complaints

177

about cleaning ladies no good either. 'I love mine,' she says in a voice that wrong foots me on the instant. I mean, I suppose I've grown fond of Maria, the gardener's wife, after all these years she's been with us, but there are still things about her that exasperate me and/or make me laugh, enough to want to discuss them rather naughtily with other people. The way she *will* join in the conversation, for example, when she hands round the dishes, no matter who's present or what we're talking about. The way she calls Henry '*Sor'Conte*' which sounds so peculiar, verging on the obscene. The way she smothers everything, but everything, in garlic, even egg mousse, even sole; the time she told us her brother-in-law, who suffers from heart trouble, was having a Black and Decker put in his chest, when what she meant (presumably) was a pacemaker . . .

I love mine. Said as if she's talking about a close relative or someone. What can you reply to that? Nothing, it slaps you into silence. I mean, affection, yes, but love and cleaning ladies don't quite go together, not in my repertoire. Then one day last week, while we were sitting side by side during a rehearsal, watching Henry trying to get Isobel Marcucci to do whatever it was he wanted (I was reminded of a lion tamer with a very tricky lion), we looked at one another and got the giggles simultaneously, and that was that. We went off to have a cup of coffee together and then bitched for ages about pretty well everyone in the show who deserved it. Which made three as far as I was concerned, and three for her too, but not quite the same three. Friends from then on.

So now I know why Henry likes her company so much, and don't resent it a bit: once you get past the roughness, she's nice, and amusing too. Perhaps, just perhaps, she could be a little bit lesbian, but I've never minded that, being so much the opposite way myself, in fact I think it's rather flattering. I must tell Misa this next time we talk, to reassure her.

And now I'm going to go and lie by the pool and run through my lines again, like a proper actress. It strikes me that perhaps I should have *been* an actress, I seem so cut out for it somehow. Now that's a thought.

*ORSO MARIA – RECITATIVE WITH PENCIL ON A SMALL SQUARE PACKET

My own *piccolina*. Mobile phone not working, alas. Having difficulty reaching you on yours too. Perhaps it has fallen sick out of sympathy? Full of work up to my ears, even in August – oh, my God, what a life. Till our next meeting, here is a little golden something to hang round your pretty neck and remind you of all the happy times we have spent together. You say you're sad, please don't be, can't bear to think of you being sad. Just remember, whatever happens, you will always be my *special* little love. Promise me that?

AMABILE — ARIA

I've done it now. It slipped out, I knew it would. Well, I couldn't really help it, I had to say something. Giovanna was ranting against him that hard. I've rung him, Amabile, she said. I didn't want to, and you know I didn't, but for Lucia's sake I swallowed my pride and rang him to ask for help and, vain old billygoat egoist that he is, he hasn't bothered to do anything yet at all. I'm so ashamed of him, I hardly know what to say. The other business is nothing in comparison, I've got used to it, but I've always thought that in a fix – if any of us really needed him – his generous side would come to the fore. And now I find . . .

And off she went with some very harsh words against him that he really doesn't deserve, poor man, or not on this account anyway. So I told her about him coming over in secret like that and collecting all the paperwork and asking us not to breathe a word. Real Christian charity, I said, no show about it at all.

He did that? she said. I could see the news startled her, but it was out now, and there was no calling it back. Amabile, look me in the eyes: he really and truly did that? When? How? What did he do exactly? What did he say? How long did he stay with you? What time was it when he arrived? What time was it when he left? Perhaps it's only wishful thinking (and perhaps it's selfish of me too – wanting to keep the household together so that I don't lose my job), but I've got a feeling she was upset he'd been so close and hadn't been round to see her, and didn't want it to show.

Having said the main thing I thought I might as well say everything, so I did. Even about the insurance, and about him wanting no payment.

Cunning bastard, Giovanna said when I'd finished. Cunning, cunning, cunning, cunning, bastard, bastard, bastard, bastard. She repeated it so many times I lost count. But the way she spoke was different now, angry and forgiving together – a bit like I get myself, I suppose, when the boys do something terrible that's meant well, and you don't know whether to praise or scold. These last days she's worked herself up into a bit of a state again. Ashtrays all over the place this morning, and the studio – looks like monkeys have been in there. All those lovely costumes, all that lovely material – I could hardly believe my eyes. I thought to begin with it must have been done by an intruder out of spite. Last year, when Felice the quarry boss went and built himself a swimming pool – and why shouldn't he, I say, he works hard enough, and gives work to plenty more – someone went and tipped in a cartload of cow muck overnight. Had to empty all the water out, and then the mayor rationed the running water and it was September before he could start filling it up again. Ready for skating, pretty well.

But no, she did it herself. Can you believe it. On purpose. They'll look lovely on the stage, she said, these fringey bits, they'll catch the light beautifully. I didn't want things to look too pretty pretty, Amabile, know what I mean? I wanted a harsh note.

Well, she's got that all right, and I reckon she'll get a harsh note too from those who've got to wear the stuff. The

Contessa from Montaldo Castle is playing a role, so I hear, that pretty young woman Stefano used to drive for and whose name I could never pronounce. Tarsca, Tirsca. I can't see *her* appearing in public dressed like a scarecrow. She's very particular: Stefano always shaved before he collected guests for her, even if it was evening time. I think he fancied her a bit, quite honestly. I wonder if she felt the same way about him? He *was* so good-looking, better than Beppe and me put together. It's terrible to think that now . . .

But I won't dwell on those things any more. I don't need to. Lucia's got her meeting with the judge tomorrow, and today I woke up thinking of that, and only that, and didn't come round to Stefano till I went in to call the boys and saw his football cup on the shelf. It's the first time it's happened: that I open my eyes on the day without thinking of him. That cup's getting tarnished, must give it a clean some time.

Then there's the show tomorrow night. Pity about the time because there's a film on television the boys wanted to watch, but I can't let Giovanna down, we'll all have to go, like it or not. I suppose I could leave them with their grandma at a pinch, but I'd be that worried about what I'd find when I got back, it'd take all the pleasure away. I don't know that I'll make much out of it as it is – opera's a bit long-winded for me, all that gargling. Pavarotti and 'O Sole Mio' is about my limit, and even then I think the fatness is distracting. I keep on wondering how he keeps his trousers up, and how that young girl he's taken up with can stomach all that – well, stomach. No business of mine. That blind man, too, I like listening to him, and he sings serious songs – classical. But a whole opera . . .

Still, it'll be sitting down, and there'll be the scenery, and halfway through there's a break and we can go and get some ices in the bar and have a bit of a natter with the couple that run it – friends of Paola's, they are, but with none of her restlessness, more old-fashioned like, they've even left the old wooden counter in place, which Paola says is unhygienic but I think is nice. I might settle Beppe in there straightaway, that'd be an idea, he'll only nod off anyway when the music starts. And I might go one further still and drop the boys off on arrival at the Montaldo football pitch. They'd be much happier kicking a ball around with the other youngsters, and I could take a little stool with me and put my feet up and have a real good rest. Lay my head back, pretend I was at the beauty parlour. My first night out since . . . well, since Fabio was born, it must be. Lucia's mother could never be relied on for baby-sitting, flighty old trollop, forgive my tongue, so it was always me. But there was no sacrifice in it – giving a break to Stefano, that's all it was. Only wish now I had given him more. Can't do much now, can I? Keep my fingers crossed for Lucia tomorrow, look after the boys . . . But for him himself?

Look after yourself a bit too, Mother, that's what he would say. If you really want to put a smile on my face, take a little care of yourself too, do it for my sake. We were that close, I can hear him saying it. But the way I'm made it's the most difficult thing of all.

Still. Who knows? People change. I might try. I bought that encyclopaedia, didn't I, and that was with myself in mind. *And* I used up the old lady's money and went and collected it. One of these days, when the boys are older and Lucia's settled down and all the debts are paid off, I might try. And I mean it.

HENRY –
BRIEF ROMANCE AND ARIA

. . . its power had gone; it had taken a nose dive.

And yet, and yet. Who is to say that the human brain does not work better in some sectors without its reasoning equipment? The cold part, the hard part, the dry ratiocinative lobelet with its syllogistic skeleton poking through: igitur, ergo, q.e.d. – *why should this be the champion arbiter and not, say, the pillowy, squashy bit which dents at the note of the nightingale?*

Napier . . .

Napier. Napier. Who gives a snake's shoulderblade for Napier? Would it help if I changed his abominable literary name? Of course it wouldn't, there's nothing wrong with the name, in fact it's rather a nice one; it's the novel that stinks. Or that sucks, as Emi corrects me. This novel sucks. All novels my brain is capable of fathering suck. Perhaps all novels of the future suck *tout court*. The trusty old story-teller with his weft of words strung over a paper warp has lost his job to the new fellow with the screen and the pictures. Woyzek always wrung my heart, poor man: a wig-maker just when wigs were on the out, you could see he was headed for disaster. And now I follow in his worn-out shoes: a fiction writer when there is no more call for written fiction, no more justification for it either, and when no one wants to have anything to do with the stuff bar write it to show off. A dying trade. A dead one. Time to dig a mass grave for the stillborn embryos of human vanity and put a headstone over it: Late Twentieth-Century Novel in All its Manifestations. R.I.P. (Except, no, no need: with the dreadful glut in production the late twentieth-century novel has already buried itself. What else are bookshops nowadays except vast paper tumuli; mounds of literary corpses with the odd live victim, maybe, underneath, struggling in vain to get out?)

Napier put his head in his hands and thought . . . Thought nothing. There is no Napier, there never was, there never will be. He has no hands, poor bastard, he has no head and *a fortiori* no thoughts inside it. If I were rich enough in human terms, if I were generous enough to distribute my riches, I could perhaps force him into being. Golem him, jump-start him, give him my blood, my sweat, my skin and tissues and then blow my breath into him, Phwooh. Only then would he live on the page, and probably limply at that. But the process is painful and quite frankly, *entre nous*, what would be the point? Dross-seekers have the movies: our entertainment factories churn them out in daily droves. Gold-seekers, those few there are, rightly prefer biographies, diaries, letters, the odd poem maybe – places where the real human voice can be heard cutting a real human record that *tells* you something. Worth knowing. For example . . .

Boswell on Johnson: *This reminds me of the ludicrous account which he gave Mr Langton, of the despicable state of a young Gentleman of good family. 'Sir, when I heard of him last, he was running about town shooting cats.' And then in a sort of kindly reverie, he bethought himself of his* own favourite cat, and said, 'But Hodge shan't be shot; no, no, Hodge shall not be shot.' Magic. There he is, the magnetic old fart, with his cat on his grease-stained paunch, alive, alive-o.

Lady Mary Wortley Montague to Lady Tiddlypush or whoever: *The curate, indeed, is very filthy. Such a red, spongy, warty nose. Such a squint! In short, he is ugly beyond expression; and what ought naturally to render him peculiarly displeasing to one of Mrs D's constitution and propensities, he is stricken in years. Nor do I really know how they will live. He has but forty-five pounds a year – she but a trifling sum; so that they are likely to feast upon love and ecclesiastical history, which will be very empty food without a proper mixture of beef and pudding.*

The same writer in a translation of an epitaph and a quite different mood: *We come into this world, we lodge and we depart. He never dies that's lodged within my heart.*

Augustine of Hippo on the death of a friend: *My eyes looked everywhere for him, but he was not there to be seen. I hated all the places we had been together, because he was not in them and they could no longer whisper to me, 'Here he comes!' as they would have done had he been alive but absent for a while. I had become a puzzle to myself, asking my soul again and again, 'Why are you downcast?' 'Why do you drag me down with you?' But my soul had no answer to give. If I said, 'Wait for God's help,' she did not obey. And in this she was right because, to her, the well-loved man who she had lost was better and more real than the shadowy being in whom I would have her trust. Tears alone were sweet to me, for in my heart's desire they had taken the place of my friend.*

Byron's letters to Lady Melbourne, Marcus Aurelius's to Fronto: *So we had supper after we had bathed in the oil-press room – I don't mean we bathed in the oil-press room, I mean we had supper there after we had bathed – and enjoyed ourselves no end listening to the locals having a dig at each other* . . . (That hasn't worn too bad, either, over its two thousand odd years.) Waugh's to Mitford, Madame de Sévigné's to her daughter; the great essayists – Bacon, Strachey; the great diarists, among whom I almost number, rather incongruously after what I've said, Adrian Mole . . . I could go on quoting them for months on end and still come up with winners. How can the miserable Napier hold his head up in such company? How can he dare to show his imitation nose? Put your scribbler's kit away, Henry, stop sullying pages, even electronic pages. If it's a question of *vivi o scrivi*, *vivi* for God's sake, *vivi* before it's too darn late. Go for it. Get back in that car of yours that brought you so begrudgingly homewards yesterday evening, start it up, turn its nose in the right direction, and go for it. And not tomorrow either – today *is* fucking tomorrow and it's nearly over anyway – but now, understand me, NOW. Those headlights you crossed by the bridge – low-slung, yellowy, prowly – didn't like the look of them, no, didn't like the look of them at all.

ORSO MARIA – DUET WITH ANSWERPHONE

– Thanks for calling. Please leave a message after the beep.
    – Fox cub, fox cub. I don't care about my promises, I can't keep them any more. Don't switch the tape off or run out of the room or whatever you do when you hear my voice, there's something I just have to tell you. I love you, that's what. You know I love you, don't you? I love you and I can't live without you and nothing else and nobody else counts.

Fox cub? Volpettina? Are you there listening? I don't expect you to do anything about this, I just want you to know. OK? Good-night, my love, my old true love, my only.

EMILY – RECITATIVE IN E-MAIL

mipsy porker mine love you too much to wish you were here but selfishly i do/this week not so bad because we have this show of henry's on I told you about – this mozart lark – which means at least we'll see some new faces even if it's only locals jeering but otherwise life's as flat as fffing fettuccine

old hen is sweet but ditchwater gaia hasn't got a braincell that isn't occupied by clothes or flowers or healthfoods or diets or whatever the bung (for bungalow you silly – no top storey) never rings and I can't blame him as he knows the pheotus – no not right either never mind – isn't his now I told him before he left I thought I'd better real pa never rings either the prick but there again it's partly my fault because him I *haven't* told and now we're on the subject should i do you think? tell him and then face the consequences which might mean divorce and marriage and publicity and all sort of hassle get your sharp little neurones into that one *maialina* which means little pig in italian what with learning my part and chatting up the lighting technician at least at least my italian is benefiting from this washout summer

e

LOUISE — PAEAN
ON A RE-CONNECTED PC

Martin – A few lines just to let you know I'll be flying back after all on the 31st as arranged. No way I could change the date – first week of September for some reason is really popular, perhaps it's the Jubilee looming. Never mind, my fault, should have done it earlier. Sorry I was so aggressive over the phone the other evening but in some ways you're worse than your father was. I earn the stuff, for God's sake, what I do with my money is my affair. Or not? Besides, it's not a broken-down stable, it's a dear little antique stone house, dating back centuries, on the ground floor of which animals *were once stabled*. Big difference. OK there's no running water at present but there's a well looks nice and soggy, and pipes can be laid and water brought. Same for the road and the electric. It's not a lousy investment either, it's a very good investment, and the Marcuccis are not trying to get me to share their misery, quite the opposite, they're letting me in on their little corner of heaven. And lastly I am not mad and menopausal, I'm doing the first really sane thing in ages, that's all.

Love from your happy old pasta-eating, vino-drinking, garlic-smelling, snake-loving, opera-going, truffle-packing

Momma

JOANNA — RONDO

A day of such chaotic flurry that I hardly know where to start. Costumes to be driven over to the bar in Montaldo, where they've set up a kind of actors' dressing room for us in the billiard room (memo: take a decent-size mirror too while I'm about it). Those special fluorescent green stage lights to be collected from the Bevagna theatre (*if* they've got them like the man said, bet they haven't). Boots for Elvira to be found somewhere, she can't be the only one without – or wellies at a pinch. Sequences to be run through again with the old fellow who Federico found to scene-shift for us . . . German name . . . Fritz, that's right, Fritz. Rows to be sustained with probably everyone, but in particular with cross old Floss once she sees the touches I've added to her precious frillies . . .

All this on my plate and what am I doing? It's nine o'clock, and I'm lying in bed, every nerve in my body slack, gazing at the ceiling and waiting for Orso to bring me a cup of really strong breakfast coffee. It's so long since he's done it he's probably forgotten the way I like it and where the coffee's kept, but he can't ask, and I can hear him clattering around in the kitchen like a well-behaved but dogged guest. No Amabile to help him, because today's the day Lucia's got her hearing with the judge and she and Beppe have set off at dawn in their church clothes to bring her support. Keep fingers crossed for that, although Orso says not to worry, it's a foregone conclusion they'll save her from jug and send her to the rehabilitation centre instead. Cheaper: they work their junkies to the bone here in practical-minded Umbria.

So, anyway, there it is. I've waved no formal white flag as yet but inside me I've half relented again, taken him halfway back, or taken myself halfway back to him, whichever is the best description. Probably neither: while he held me in his arms last night, begging forgiveness, swearing eternal love and fidelity from now on, the sense of belonging was such that I knew really that neither of us had ever been away. Not totally, at any rate, only geographically, only on the map. Oh, God, the smell of him, what a soothing effect it has on my foolish old nostrils . . . like breathing witch hazel. The way our bodies fit together, the way they stay interlocked like the best intarsia work, even on the verge of sleep when a person usually craves solitude and kicks all interlopers away. I thought I picked up traces of home in Henry's voice, and it may have been so, up to a point, but smell and touch strike at a deeper level than hearing. Home is not so much where your ear is as where your nose is, where your flesh and skin and nerves are. Orso's bed has been a bed of nails for me through the years, and of nettles and all sorts of irritants, but it is my nest, my berth, it is the socket I plug into and from which all my energies derive. (WRITE THIS DOWN SOMEWHERE in case at some future date you get fed up again and forget it. IT'S NO USE GOING OFF ANYWHERE. THIS BED YOUR CENTRE IS etc. etc. bla bla.)

A car swept in as we lay there – a crunch of gravel, a quick swirl of light across the window – and then swept out again. Henry? Surely not, probably just someone taking a wrong turn. But if it was Henry, that puts the lid on it, double tight. Orso didn't appear to notice, but I think this was studied behaviour: he's asked me some very piercing questions this morning about what I've been doing during his absence, who I've been seeing, why I'm out so much, why I've gone through so much wine. Absurd in a way, but he is the jealous one now. And so I think he will remain. I am beyond jealousy: I have passed it like you pass an exam and I know I won't have to sit for it again, ever – not this one. Something's gone from my side of the relationship as a result, worn away like the tension in a piece of knicker elastic exposed to too much stress, but something else has taken its place. Something thinner and tougher. I don't need him any more as a prop for my balance, I think that's what it is: I am fond of him and am content, even glad, to live with him, but I no longer need him. I stay upright on my own. And that is why I can take him back the way I'm doing: because I'm no longer in danger of falling.

No one will know this, of course. I didn't know it myself until now. To the world, to Orso himself, I will continue to be the Elvira of the situation, the incurable *innamorata*, the mug, the softie; only I will be aware of my strength. Will this bother me? Not a bit. Strength can be worn any old how: back to front, next to the skin, between your jeans and your long-johns; as with a fur lining, the important thing is, not to flaunt it but to have it. The rest is just birdseed.

Claudia will be furious, she was re-living her own battles through me, she'll think I've let her down, caved in, exposed her to defeat by proxy. Vicky will be relieved perhaps on her own account, but troubled on mine: she too will think I've yielded and come out yet again the loser. Henry?

Henry, I don't know. This soft spot I think he has for me – I may just have been imagining it, or at any rate imagining it to be much softer than it is. Or was. Or might have been. Wounded vanity can play you a lot of tricks that way: someone gives you a smile and a bit of their time, and straight away you chalk them up as an admirer. Pathetic really. No, I don't think Henry will be much affected either one way or the other; I hope not anyway, he's such a pet, he doesn't deserve to suffer so much as a twinge on my account. (Nor I on his, but in some strange way I do. Nothing I can formulate really, just a small noise, a small disturbance, as if there were a little marooned castaway inside me crying out faintly, Oy, oy, oy, Henry, I'm here, don't leave me, take me with you.) The only person to be straightforwardly pleased and no complications will be Amabile, and even she, subconsciously, in a little suffragette corner of her brain, may think I've been a bit of a wimp: all that talk of independence and then the moment Orso beckons, tears and hugs and scurry! into his arms again. They're pretty feminist really, these Umbrian women, behind their traditional gallant-little-wifey façades. And no wonder when they work longer hours than the men, and make all the decisions, and invest the savings and draw up the budget and do practically everything except choose the make of the car, and sometimes that as well. Beppe bangs down his glass on the table every time he wants more wine or water – toc, toc, in silence, no please, no thank you – and Amabile fills it up for him without a murmur, but it's a formal atavistic gesture like a bird's parade of feathers, I'm the cock, you're the hen; means nothing on the power plane, nothing at all.

Oh, men. (Never thought I would catch myself saying that, in that way, like my mum's charlady, but here I am.) Why is it they market themselves so much better than we do? It's as bad as French and Italian cheeses – the Italian ones with all the variety, all the substance, all the freshness and the goodness and the value and the taste, and the scurvy French ones with their plastic rinds and laboratory moulds getting all the praise. Between men and women who are the vainer? Who are the gossips? Who are the more irrational? Who the more incapable of separating sex and sentiment? On my findings there's no contest. Look at Orso with his affairs – would a woman with his needs ever get into such tangles? She would not, she would screw, and tell whoever she was screwing with to keep quiet about it and get no fancy ideas in his head, and keep quiet about it herself. Men may fantasise about the zipless fuck or whatever it's called, but it's only women who go in for it. 'Shut up, Benjamin,' as Mrs Robinson said to the garrulous Graduate in the aftermath of sex. You'd never catch Orso saying that to any of his girlfriends, he'd be more likely to want to discuss poetry.

I read somewhere – some music critic or other in a courtly mood – that life is a journey towards Mozart. It'd be nice if it was. It seems to me more of a journey towards cliché. When you're young you fight against all received opinion, spit it out like fibre: Children *don't* need discipline, Criminals *don't* need punishing, Man is *not* warlike, Greed is *not* inborn, High culture is *not* for an élite, The gulf between the sexes is *not* unbridgeable. Only old people assert the contrary, failed old miserygutses who've loused things up and are looking to shift the blame; we will show them better.

And, no, we *won't* think the same when we get to their age, that's the biggest lie of all. Then, like cud, you spend the rest of your life chewing on these rejected pellets of information, stuffing them down your gullet and trying not to choke on them.

The gulf between the sexes *is* unbridgeable. I've digested that one now. Which is not to say you can't get across it, a bridge is not the only way of spanning a gulf, but there is no convenient or permanent thoroughfare to take you to and fro: only the mind-athletes can make it, and only when they're on top form. For some of them, too, the effort is so great they can't make the leap back again but get stuck on the other side.

Anyway, enough blathering. Get cracking, you ninny. A show – it's funny but it takes precedence over all else. I was talking through my hat when I said amateur theatricals were only for the rich and bored: I hadn't pondered the question enough. You've only got to think of how people in extreme situations like sieges and internment camps club together to stage an entertainment: it's not for the spectators, it's for those taking part. Gives them something to think about that while it lasts is more engaging of the mind than captivity or terror or death itself. My life is at a turning point – if I don't make the break now I never will, and if I give in now it is for ever: I will have used up all my leverage – plus which I am worried for Amabile's sake, worried about Vicky flying back, which she does on Thursday, worried about the catalogue not being ready on time, worried that the last painting I've been working on for the exhibition is not up to standard, or only curate eggily in parts: it shows signs of the summer's stress, and can you wonder; I'm worried about all these things, and yet I can think of nothing worse in the arc of today's happenings than that our show should be a flop. So go to it, lazybones, out of bed and get your rollerblades on. I don't like to have to admit this, but with Orso in my life again, the current is flowing at high voltage and I feel I can do anything, anything . . .

HENRY − LAMENT

That's that, then. To wake, perchance to stop sodding off into dreamland. The malevolent car was there, crouching in the darkness like a preying feline. Get out of here, you trespasser, I got here first, the prize is mine. I have never hated a machine so much, and I have hated a lot of machinery in my time, starting with my very first electric engine, which I washed in caustic soda out of an excess of cleaning zeal and ruined utterly and had to hide from my father thereafter. 'Bring out that train of yours, Henry. Where's it got to?' The words would make me sweat blood. The Duchess of Atholl, it was called. I am glad the last Duke was celibate and that there was no Duchess of Atholl my contemporary, she would have made me sweat blood too, in remembrance.

So. My golden summer. A gilded mirage, that's all it was in the end. My dragon a chimera, myself the laughable old slug of always − slow, blind, wavering, an intrinsically ground-based creature, lacking spring, lacking propulsion. Henry, no, Henry never needed unbouncing in my mother's view, and paradoxically in my case it was not a compliment: How lucky, she used to proclaim briskly to those surrounding her, myself included, how lucky he's not an elder son. Fantasies. Faint little fugues. Useless to recriminate about delay: if only, if only; I never would have done anything anyway. I would have driven in, the way I did, drooled a bit at the steering wheel over hypothetical enterprise, hypothetical reward, hypothetical happiness ever after, and driven out again. Back to Gaia and my everyday yoke to which I have become so inured that its irksomeness is hardly an issue. That is my destiny, that is the way I am made. It takes courage and energy to direct life's flow into your own runnels, and I have never been strong in either suit.

Only one thing I did last night that I can be in any way proud of, and that was to wake Gaia on my re-entry and make love to her with the intention of giving her what she so desperately wants and needs: a child. I stood looking at her for a long time before I roused her. She is not a pretty sleeper, her face needs muscle control to acquire its beauty, and this fact, this shortcoming, touched me far deeper than perfection would have done. I saw lurking under her features the woman she could become, and that she will become for certain if I continue to deny her the softening influence of motherhood – a handsome, slightly leathery, slightly jowly *domina*, of the kind of which her native Venice is full; a blue-rinsed, bejewelled bridge-player like her mum, all elegance and glaze but with a perennial pleat of dissatisfaction plucking at the otherwise perfect mouth, pulling it awry.

I knew in that moment that I loved her, was concerned enough, involved enough, responsible enough to want to arrest the development of this *Unterfrau*, this harpy. Choke, bitch, I thought, and laid myself over her, stifling her with a long insidious kiss. Gaia, my Gaia, my old, happy teetotum Gaia, who rights herself at the flip of a finger, awoke under me, as if resuscitated by a rescuer administering the kiss of life (which, who knows, it may

206

well turn out to be) and gave me a lightning-flash smile. How much easier it is to make happy people happy. When she realised what I was up to, instead of complying she begged me to stop since she had recently been so careless about taking the pill – *sbadata* was the word she used, implying a slight confession as well as a description – that the doctor had now taken her off it entirely in order to reset her cycle. 'So it's a very bad time, see, Enrichetto.'

There were such lashings of generosity in this, and of honesty as well, that I felt a flare-up of my old passion for her, and a corresponding flare-down of any passion whatsoever for myself, bar scorn. I lied to myself when I said she didn't love me: she loves me, God knows why. I had thought her not only capable but actually guilty of cheating, when if anything . . . in thoughts at least . . .

So, No, my sweet, I said, it's a very good time, the best we're likely to have. And with that she beamed at me again like a lighthouse and I went ahead and crossed my private Rubicon. I don't want another child, I am much too old to be a willing father, admitted that such a being exists, but in a case like this *vieillesse oblige*. I cannot have Gaia turning into an elegant old sourpuss on my account. If I can't provide her with fulfilment myself, at least I can do it this way, through *interposta persona*. Not the best of reasons for bringing a new life into the world, but there are many worse. A daughter – even in my present collapsed-soufflé state I can see there might be special consolations in that, and there is a fifty–fifty chance. I would be tempted to call her Giovanna, but I seem to remember Gaia always being set on Benedetta. A blessing. Fine by me. Benedict quite acceptable too.

The years, which fell off me at the start of this folly, have crowded back again, more and heavier than before. Dignity should by rights have returned with them, but of that I see no trace. Laughing clown or moping clown – still clown I am. Oh, Christ, the fatigue of it all.

> Scarcely a tear to shed;
> Hardly a word to say;
> The end of a summer day;
> Sweet love dead.

Only for love read neurosis, and for end read beginning. (Or read nothing: I'm fed up with this poetry kink of mine. Every emotion comes to me trailing behind it a dusty old tail of other people's words. What are they there for? To act as padding, create a decoy action, what?) Sixteen hours at the inside, sixteen clamouring, hammering hours to get through before I can be alone again with my spleen. If the night is fine and for some incalculable reason we find favour with our public, then it could be even longer. Together with the dreaded local wine that circulates on such occasions I will have to down all sorts of bitter draughts: Joanna on the arm of her risible Don Giovanni, who I have no doubt will have slid his oily way into her life again. (And her heart. And her bed. Oh, God, the lights were out when I got there last night; the house was still; that's where he was all right, that's the place his kind makes for always – those alcove boys, how well they know their way around.) The parody of her plight, played out on the stage. And played abominably, what is worse. I know the whole thing is so lamentably weak it will not even invite laughter, merely tedium. Tedium, that is, once the initial bafflement over Joanna's stage design has worn off: the wires and whatnots may be good for a few minutes' titters-cum-shock. God knows what she's done to the costumes; she's only had them in her keeping for forty-eight hours, can't have inflicted that much damage, or can she?

Anyway, it all ties in with a nice specific precision: bungling breeding bungling, failure breeding failure. A small success in the context of the larger débâcle would have been more difficult to deal with. This way there will be no smiles, no after-theatre camaraderie, no back slapping. We foreigners will climb into our clapped-out station wagons, and the locals will climb into their immaculate new Range Rovers, and the evening will end in so many puffs of exhaust fumes. Phutt, phutt, phutt.

And she – the one responsible? She will climb into the obnoxious Porsche, the door will slam shut, and as it does so some aperture in my heart will slam shut too, sealing off for ever the fount of whatever emotion it was that has flowed so freely and bizarrely over these past weeks. Call it what you like – romantic love, romantic lust, infatuation or simple late-day fling of ageing genes – it has dripped its last drops; time now to pull the chain on it and make way for the sanitising flush of Lethe.

*GAIA − RECITATIVE WITH LAPTOP

Misa − You wanted the recipe for Patricia Lante's cordial. At last I have managed to get if from her, cagey old frump, although I'd think it's too late now, even where you are, to find elderflowers in blossom.

Funny, today is the day of the opera and we should be running around in circles, Henry especially, but we are dead calm and lazy: me and Emi sunning ourselves by the pool, and Henry inside in his study, listening to music. It being the big day of the village *festa*, the servants have all been given the day off, and I can hear the telephone ringing and ringing inside the house and can't be bothered to answer it. Hope it's not you. Henry's closer but he doesn't seem that bothered either. Misetta, *we are both very happy*, tell you why when I see you.

Remember how Mammà always said that husbands get more and more difficult the older they get? Well, with Henry thank God it's not that way at all. OK, he's been through this andropause thing recently or whatever it's called, but quite honestly it hasn't lasted much longer than the measles, and now that he's over it we're stronger and closer as a couple than we've ever been. Marriage is a journey, no? Do you find that with Astolfo? It's a journey − a sea voyage perhaps − and I feel we've been through choppy waters and have now entered a wonderful calm sunny harbour. And don't mock and say I'm being whimsical: I've so much to tell you but it can wait until London. Oh what fun that will be. Perhaps we ought to invite old Brissie to join us there? What do you think? A bit of a lead weight but she *would* so enjoy it, and when you're happy I think you should try to spread your happiness, don't you?

Incidentally, Emi has just told me a rather surprising piece of news, that you're not to repeat, or not yet, or not to anyone outside the family. It seems that the real father of the baby is not the Wolfgang creature at all, but a famous press baron, dotty about her apparently and oozing money and old enough to be her father. This just shows that Astolfo is right, and that members of the English aristocracy, no matter how low they fall, always fall on their blazoned feet. I am pleased about this, as it *was* a slightly embarrassing project, having to introduce the craggy *montanaro* to people here in Italy as 'family' – even the good looks were a bit overdone, if you know what I mean, and the grammar . . . *non ci facci caso*!

Oh I *am* so small-minded, it's awful. Henry on the other hand will not be pleased, as in his view a penniless hillbilly with kind eyes and shy manners ranks above a pluri-divorced press magnate, who he's sure to dismiss as dubious and pushy and after Emi's lustre. And this is another funny thing about the English aristocracy: that about certain social distinctions they honestly don't give a fig. Or understand a fig either: it's as if they were stuck in a time warp round about the reign of King Arthur. Someone told me the Japanese are much the same, but I bet they're more realistic. Nothing wrong with pushiness or money – think of the Medici, think of the Agnelli. Quite, Henry would say, quite. I despair.

Anyway, to more practical matters. Here's what you asked for: You take twenty-eight heads of elderflower, eight spoonfuls of sugar, a sliced lemon, one and a half spoonfuls of citric acid, shove them in a bucket, cover them with two and a half litres cold boiled water, and leave to soak for forty-eight hours, then strain and bottle. Is that all? That's all. This is an upper-class English recipe and the upper-class English are pretty slack about housekeeping too, most of them. We went to dinner with some really grand neighbours last week, just over the border into Tuscany, and the house was crawling with ticks. Two fell off the ceiling on to the table as we were eating. Must get some more dogs, our hostess said, totally unfazed and not the shadow of an apology, they'll mop them up in no time. Just imagine Mammà – she'd have had a stroke!

Must stop now and get some clothes on. Henry's just come out with a huge jug of Pimm's and a hunted expression and says he's taking us out to lunch. Right over near the Lake of Corbara somewhere, so that nobody can find us, and by the time we're back all the last-minute hitches will have sorted themselves out. There's the true English spirit again. Isn't he marvellous? Oh, I do love him.

Baci, bacioni, bacetti,
G.

CANON ON AN ANSWERPHONE

– Henry, Friday morning, ten o'clock. Near as makes no difference, anyway. This is Florence. Where are you? I need to speak to you. We've a real crisis on our hands. That friend of yours, little Miss Picasso or whoever she thinks she is, has gone and . . . Oh, too complicated to explain over the machine. Ring me back, will you, the moment you get this message? Urgent.

– Henry? Florence. Twenty-past ten. Not a squeak from you yet. Where are you? What are you doing? Where's Gaia? Where's Emily? Ring me, for God's sake, things are serious.

– *Signor Conte. Federico here, Federico Baciucco from Elettro Center. You know: Masetto. I'm sorry to bother you in your home, Signor Conte, but we've got a bit of a problem up here with the fire inspectors. They say the cables for the footlights are dangerous the way they are and we've got to string them in the air and pass them over the audience's heads. Regulations. If you ask me, they're just being awkward: they're from Gualdo and they've got something on tonight as well, some Latin American dance contest. Lambada. Macarena. What should I do? There's no pole we can fix the cables to. I've asked the Mayor if we can put one up specially for the purpose but the trouble is . . . Beep, beep, beep.

– Henry? Henry? Florence again. How come you don't answer if your number is engaged? Are you hiding behind

215

that machine? Henry? *Henry*? Shit, I think he's really out. Henry, don't play possum with me, it's a total calamity: all that work, all that beautiful material – it's totally, totally unusable. I don't think you realise. No one could unless they saw it. We'll have to contact a place that rents theatrical costumes or something, and . . . Oh, heck, the only place I know is in Foligno and it's shut for the whole of August. Henry, for God's sake, ring me, think of something, do something.

– *Still me, Signor Conte. Federico. Masetto. I'm sorry, the tape ran out, and then the line was busy. It's like this: the Mayor says the Belle Arti people will kick up a fuss if we erect a pole. The square's a national treasure, he says, under their protection. I said what about drilling a hook into the church tower and one in the gate opposite and slinging a wire across. He says that'd be worse. I said, who'd ever notice in the dark? But elections are coming up, and he's a windy fellow, is Capogrossi. I asked what he wanted us to do then, attach the cables to a floating balloon? Signor Conte, see if you can come up with some solution, talk Capogrossi round or something, it's half-past ten and time's running sho . . . Beep, beep, beep.

– Monday, 10.45 a.m. Message for Lord Thirsk. Henry, Isobel speaking. Look, I don't know what's going on, my phone's not one hundred per cent dependable, so maybe you've been trying to contact me and failing, but I've had a stressful call from Florence, which has upset both Milton and me considerably. She accuses you of treason, sabotage, pillory, favouritism, all sorts of crimes, and I just hope, for your sake and ours, you'll be able to clear yourself. What concerns me most is that from what she says it seems

216

Milton – who may I remind you is a leading academic in the States, which to us poor ex-colonials *means* something, believe it or not – is required to appear on stage dressed in . . . Beep, beep, beep.

– Sorry, you have a real short loop there, I'm having difficulty compressing. Look, I think you'll agree with me. I'm sure Florence got it wrong, because Joanna Volpi is pretty zany, it's true, but she normally has a certain style the way she does things. However, *if* the rumour's true, and Milton's outfit is the way Florence describes, then I think you'll agree that some kind of corrective action needs taking – like *now* – and you're the only one can take it. Don't think I'm overreacting – or do, if you like, it's no big deal either way – but we have lawyer friends in this country as well as in the States, and if as a result of his appearance in your show there is any tarnishing of Milton's public image, then we may be the ones to take action, and I mean it.

– Henry, this is not remotely funny any more. Henry, where the hell have you got to? It's not only the costumes now, it's everything. Your precious Volpi woman has brought over a bootload of boots in her car – I mean a carload of . . . well, you know what I mean – which she expects everyone to wear. Showing, with their clothes tucked into the tops, even the women. And some ghastly psychedelic lights or whatever they're called, the colour of bile. *And* there's some kind of problem over the electric, and everyone's in a fuss, and the Mayor's having rabies. I'm backing out of this, I'm resigning, I want nothing more to do with it, I want my name taken off the programme. If I don't hear from you by lunchtime I'm . . . Beep, beep, beep.

– *Dottor Tirsk, this is Gabriella from the Comune

calling. The Mayor's anxious to get in touch with you on an important matter connected with this evening's performance. Please could you contact him on his mobile phone. He says you have the number. From midday on, if you prefer, you can find him in person at the crossing by the football pitch: he's judging the cheese race.

– *Signora Tirsk. I'm Laura from Tricostile, just ringing to remind you you had an appointment with us this morning. Shampoo and body wax. We take it you're not coming in. Could you let us know, please, if you are, as today's very busy? Thanks.

– Henry? *Henry*? HENRY? Oh, this is hopeless.

– *Hello? Dottor Enrico? The other Enrico here: Enrico Capogrossi. My secretary tells me she's having difficulty getting hold of you. She says she sent someone up to the *castello* but there's no one in. Dottor Enrico, you're not walking out on us, are you? No, because we're having a spot of bother – political bother, you know, local rivalries, bit of spokes-in-the-wheels business – and what we need is a word from above, if you catch my meaning. Not right above, just – well, ministerial level would do nicely. So I was hoping that maybe you, with your contacts . . . Ring me back, Dottore, as soon as you can. The situation is serious. We Montaldini need to stick together.

– Hello? This is Orso Volpi speaking, the husband of Giovanna. I just like to say, with Giovanna we have the idea of eating a big *spaghettata* in the Molino Restaurant when the opera is finished. I invite everyone as my guests, it is my pleasure. We expect you, then, all of you. *Va bene*? OK, we look forward to seeing you. Oh, and, yes: in the wolf's mouth for this evening, eh. I like these translations of

idiomatic phrases, don't you? So funny. Of course: *di corsa.*
Non c'è di che: there is nothing of what. So, in the wolf's
mouth, and in leg everybody, ha.

   – Henry? This is unspeakable. Where is the man? Blast!
Blast! Blast!

*GAIA – FINALE

Andiamo a cenar in compagnia. That's what the sweet little fiancés – can't remember their names, Emi and electrician anyway in real life – that's what they sing at the end, and that's what we all did.

I'm not very poetical really, Henry always says I have the sensitivity of a baby armadillo where the arts are concerned, but armadillos too must have hearts under their casing, and tonight mine was touched. I don't know why. It was all so amateurish – the sets were hideous, our costumes – I can't think what had happened to them, I only know Florence was in tears at the start of things and then all pink and glowing at the end when everyone crowed round and paid her all those compliments. Brilliant, Such fun, Such a clever idea, So *witty.* Iconoclastic, said that friend of the Kleins, who it turns out is a famous New York theatre critic, and Florence, you could see, nearly peed in her panties. I don't know what it was, why it worked, but it just did.

I knew it almost from the very beginning, when my tape recorder got disconnected and, instead of hissing, all the public waited in absolute silence for Federico to hitch me up again. They were hooked already, you could tell, caught up in the little glittering booth-world of the stage. I was hooked myself. Leporello brought out the book of conquests to show me, and he was no longer that rather sour little tom puss of a man he'd been during rehearsals, fiddling with what looked like a roll of loo paper, he *was* Leporello and the book *was* the book. I got quite carried away, and the words I'd said a hundred times over, always with an effort and having to think carefully where to put the stress, came as naturally to me as if they were my own. He was false to me, the monster, he betrayed my trust. Henry, bless him, has never given me such cause for jealousy – although recently, once or twice . . . no, that's stupid – but I could feel what it was like to feel it. Not so much the Elvira of the libretto, who is too sissy for my liking, but I could imagine myself as a kind of seventeenth-century Joanna, chasing after her naughty playboy husband who scoots off every time she approaches at the wheel of his seventeenth-century Porsche. (Which I suppose would have been a carriage – a barouche, perhaps, or a landau. I must read a bit more history when I have time, it is so amusing, drawing parallels between the past and now.)

Oh, he is attractive, that husband, and what a sweet idea to offer dinner to everyone. I think he must have fed practically the whole of Montaldo in the end. Henry would have done the same, of course, and paid just as willingly, but he wouldn't have *enjoyed* it, I don't think, not in quite the same way as Orso did – or appeared to. There would have been a touch of *souffrance* in his participation. Even without the headache, which was a shame, as it meant we had to leave halfway through, but cheap wine always does that to Henry, he's built to an expensive pattern.

Anyway Orso is as cuddly as his name, a real friend of women, I would say, a real fan. I sat next to him during the meal – or half the meal, that is – and came away convinced that he not only admired me as a woman – which he

222

definitely did, you could see that a mile off, everybody could – but really liked me as a person as well, and that was more flattering still. I don't think I would like to be *married* to a man like that, I think it would be exhausting, the affairs would get you down, and I couldn't take them the way Joanna does, with her English grin-and-bear-it attitude and paint-your-way-to-peace, I'd be more inclined to scenes; but I wouldn't at all mind, *if* I were that sort of woman, having a *storia sentimentale* with him, even quite a long one. *I* would have to be the one who put an end to it, of course, because I couldn't stick the ditching either, I am far too proud. But, no, he's the sort of man whose company definitely *does* something for you, more than a new scent or a visit to a health farm. I approve.

Henry doesn't, I'm afraid, but that's because he's jealous, and I found that flattering too, it's ages since I've seen him look such daggers at another man on my account. In fact it was a pretty flattering evening – what with the clapping and the curtain calls and the Mayor presenting me with roses (I think they ought to have gone to Isobel by rights, but she got gladioli instead), and that dear Federico creature stumbling over everyone to sit next to me on the other side. (He reminds me of someone, does Federico, but I can't quite think who. Oh, yes, how silly of me, the other driver of course, the dead one, the cousin; he was rather *galante* too. Desperately unsexy, both of them, they remind me of those little Tyrolean hedgehogs people collect.) And then, to cap it all, the attentions of the suave Avvocato Volpi who is as different from a hedgehog as it is possible to be.

And all the time this glow inside, caused by the feeling – completely dotty and unfounded – that I am already

223

pregnant, already carrying Henry's child. It's all I need to make me the happiest and luckiest creature on the planet. Except, wait, no, life has given me so much, perhaps I'm that already. Armadillo casing? So what? In a world like this it strikes me it's not such a bad thing.

JOANNA – FINALE

Well, that's over, and I thought it went pretty well, all things considered. Although when you're on tenterhooks, the way I was most of the time, it's hard to judge. Old Fritz got his timing wrong and was caught in the spotlight lugging props around the stage in a huge black plastic rubbish bag and swearing his head off, but the beauty of an open-cast production like this is that nobody can really tell what's deliberate and what isn't, and I think most of the public thought his *Porco* this's and *Va'fa'* that's were part of the score. Lighting worked OK, nothing fused, nothing blew up. Actors all adequate, some more than that: Don Giovanni perfect, for example, Anna and Ottavio ghastly/brilliant, Masetto awkward but that didn't matter, Zerlina a bit weak – typical English like me, couldn't let her hair down, couldn't let go. Leporello, on the other hand, a bit too strong: Fletcher's being a professional unbalanced things slightly in my view, which was a shame. I mean, you could see he was acting – acting well, but acting – whereas the others, even Masetto with his blushes and clenched fists and ropy English, looked more like the real McCoy. Funny, should be the other way round. Gaia as Elvira was quite simply fantastic. Henry had misgivings all along, I know, but he was wrong: true, in rehearsals she'd never shown much mettle, but in front of an audience she arched her neck like a circus pony and *hoplà*! off she went. Henry himself as rigid as his niece, but in his case, being a statue, it was fine. A few hitches with the playback, and the overall sound a bit scratchy, but, no, I think, given the limitations, which were pretty crippling, it came over rather well. Clever old Henry, bet he's pleased. He didn't look it, mind you, but migraines *are* hell. And double clever to keep out of the way like that till the last minute: in Italy it's no use fussing, things always sort themselves out in the end.

Costumes, though I say it myself, were the best thing of all. I congratulated Florence on them in the interval, deadpan, and she looked deadpan back and said nothing at all, but I saw her later, during supper, mopping up praise like a sponge. 'Mad? Of course, but then I *am* a bit mad, haven't you ever noticed? Yes, Bladerunner an influence, definitely, but not only him, I think there's a touch of authentic d'Avola as well.' Silly cow. So much for liaising.

And now what? Elvira goes to a nunnery. That escape route is not open to me, so where do I go? Back to Orso, of course, but the question is how, which bits of me? Do I go back to him physically and at the same time retreat, so to speak, into a nunnery of the heart? I love a man I don't respect. (I must love him, or I wouldn't be here, grappling with the problem, would I?) Where does that leave me? It's all very well for me to tell myself that I stand on my own two feet etc. etc., that I am strong, independent, need no man, no Orso, no Henry, no masculine prop at all. The fact is, if it were true Orso wouldn't be here tonight, and I wouldn't be wrestling in my mind with what to do about him: how to square the circle of my loving him and despising him at the same time, and despising myself in consequence. I love a shit. Plenty of women love shits, shits are all the rage *chez* my undiscerning gender. What's so terrible about that?

Yes, but it's me, Joanna, we're talking about. Joanna the cool, Joanna the artist, Joanna who fancies herself no end. Not some wibbly wobbly junket of a female, all submission and forgiveness. It's me, for God's sake. Me with the proud part that paints, and who can't paint without it and can't live without painting, and who can't – daren't – ram this further wodge of humiliation down her throat for fear of suffocation.

Idea. Couldn't I treat Orso's unfaithfulness as an illness? That'd leave a loophole. I would stand by him if he had, say, a vitamin deficiency – give him his medicines and everything he needed. Couldn't I stand by him in this other trouble? Bring the girls to his bedside and hand them to him with a glass of water: one tonight, one tomorrow morning?

Nope. Grotesque. Not possible. What about consoling myself, then, with harem humbug: Wife no. 1, the constant among variables, the only woman Orso, despite his many betrayals, does not deceive, for the simple reason . . .? No, I can't do that either.

Ignore, then, play the ostrich? By all means, if he would let me, but he doesn't, he's so transparent, I read him like a book I know by heart. End of one chapter, beginning of next – I can figure out exactly where we are, even with my head under half a ton of sand.

No, there is only one way round the problem, and that is, against all odds and all reason and all experience, to believe not only that he loves me (because in his slipshod way I know he does), but to believe that this time he is sincere, and that this slightly more serious and painful episode has taught him something, and that this is and was truly the last of his escapades. It could be true, after all, just possibly. At a stretch, at a pinch. He's growing older, his pace must be slowing. And he was so contrite last night, so hard on himself, so abject. And so hard to resist. I need you, my beloved fox cub, you are everything to me, the axis of my world – without you I am lost. (Of course he needs me: where else would he find such a sucker?) Hold me close, tell me you forgive me and I swear on all that is sacred to me that I'll be a perfect husband to you from now on. (What is sacred to him, though, when his religion is conquest?) No one else matters, you know that, don't you? Just you, and Vicky, and you again, you, you, you. If you were to leave me, if anything were to happen, if you were to die before I do . . .

Sobs, tears, embraces – the heavy artillery pounding at my defences. And then, when the breach is made, in come the assault troops for the job of hand-to-hand fighting. It is all so routine, so predictable. And yet . . . Oh, hell, hell, hell. (Worked beautifully on stage, incidentally, the hell bit. I wonder if Orso was watching, I hope he was – teach him a good lesson – but I couldn't see him, I think he must have gone into the bar for cigarettes.) Hell and fire and brimstone, the thing is that I need him too, that is the truth of the matter. And since I need him, I need to believe him. And since I need to believe him, I do believe him, I genuinely do.

Oh, there'll be relapses all right, but I think – no, I'm pretty sure really – that they will be shorter and shorter, less and less messy, less and less significant, until one day they will taper off and fizzle out altogether. And even if they don't, even if he goes on to flirt with his nurse on his deathbed and with all the lady mourners at his funeral (and of those there might be quite a few), at least, at least I know we're in for a patch of quiet now, that much is certain.

And long may it last: I need a breather after all this hassle, I really do, my poor old heart feels as if it's been on a switchback. Think of that Henry business – how near I got to thinking . . . saying . . . doing . . . Honestly, life is weird, just one little signal on his part and I might have actually . . . Crazy. So be good, my Orso, be true and keep your promises and all will be well. Let me say it with priggish little Ottavio (God he looked a treat in that get-up, I never thought he'd wear it without digging in his trotters): *O mio tesoro, porgi a me un ristoro . . .*

HENRY — FINALE

Better go off and find myself a new employer, says Leporello, full of good sense as always, the moment he sees the heels of his late one disappearing down the maw of Hell and the fiery orifice snapping shut again with a gulp.

Well, that's what I'd better do: find myself some new employment. My novel? That has died an nth and ultimate death on me – more material for the flames. Philosophy? Snuffed it too, and a good thing. Wittgenstein was right: speculative thought is a malady of the brain; a neurotic attempt on the part of fussy Reason to bottle the whole magma of experience into its own set of sterile little phials. You might as well presume to put a comb to the Medusa's tresses or teach dressage to the clouds. Any real advance in knowledge can only come from Science anyway, so why bother?

What can I do to put some purpose into my life? Look after Gaia, our child if we have one, keep an eye on Peter from afar, ditto for Emi, who I fear is about to make a right shambles of her future, worse than I've done – these things go without saying. But they *don't* go without trying: ties between humans need life-blood pumping into them if they are to hold. I've been remiss about this in the past: I will improve.

What else? Translations, why not? Translating is a grossly undervalued activity, but rewarding on its own account and endlessly fascinating. (Why is it, then, that the prospect of taking my translator's hat out of mothballs and cramming it on my head again makes me cringe?) Literary criticism – plenty of work to be done there too. Criticism is in a bad way nowadays, the laws of the market have almost done for it entirely. Unputdownable. An exhilarating roller coaster of a read. Possibly the most important novel of the decade. If you have time to read only one book this year, make it this. Words fail . . . Yeah, words fail all right, how could they do otherwise when they have been milked, sucked, preyed upon, bled, vampirised to anaemia level? I've got taste, I've got judgement, contacts too, I've no axes to grind, no backs to scratch, no need to sell my soul at this particular juncture to any particular master – I think I would make rather a good critic. Cranky but good. A lone crusade, but well worth pursuing. I could go further in this doubtless unappreciated direction: I could organise a kind of lifeboat service for the few worthwhile works of fiction to be published each year (or make it lustrum), which otherwise would be submerged in the abyss. Henry's Tub, a frail little craft, no crew, no motor, no radar, but at least it might stay afloat until picked up by some larger vessel. Unfitted to produce literature myself, I could enrol myself humbly in its service. *Ma non voglio più servir, no, no, no, no, no, no, non voglio più servir . . .*

Yeah. Could. Maybe will one day, who knows, but at present I just haven't got the zip. Black dog is on me. Black dog has got me in his jaws. I have been taken up, whirled around, and now cast into the pit where the scavengers dig for morsels. I can just picture the scene on Olympus: the derisive gods lolling on their hummocks, spitting out an olive stone now and again, eager for novelty. 'Chuck that one out, Zeus. That gangly old one with the grey hair and the stoop – we've had enough of him. He was fun for a while – that "shag her with Shelley" business was hilarious – but, Hercules! they do pall on one, these humans. Can't stand it when they go all mopey. Fling him on the tip, would you, there's a good god.'

My stature is so minuscule I am uninteresting even in my pain. Losers are alleged to be the stuff of great literature – the Quixotes, the Hamlets, the Lears, the Kareninas, the Bovarys, the Fausts – but apart from a few odd-heroes-out here and there, like Svevo's Zeno and Musil's jellyfish whose name I don't even remember, they are all losers with a capital L; they lose their honour, their integrity, their loves, their lives, their souls, their all. What do I lose? Nothing, a possession that was never mine in the first place, and to obtain which I was not prepared to stretch out so much as a finger, for fear of looking oafish if spurned.

It wouldn't have worked anyway. I watched her over the supper table – for as long as I could bear it: she wouldn't have done well on the low-calorie paper diet I have to offer. Whatever it is that that smarmy trickster gives her by way of nourishment (and I think uncharitably it's mostly tripe) she evidently thrives on it: I've never seen her looking so strong, so well, so happy – curse the creep to hell along with Don Giovanni and the manuscript. But then tripe *is* more nourishing than paper, only a vegetarian bookworm like myself would disagree.

And then there's her painting, her profession – I don't *think* it would have done, when our tastes are so divergent, but it might just possibly have caused trouble, I might have been competitive, envious, resentful of her status as an artist.

Why her and not me? Or, perhaps more to the point when it indubitably *is* her and not me: Why this and not that? Whereas Creepo inhabits an aesthetic basement which keeps him comfortably below such queries. *Spassoso*, he kept on saying about Joanna's stage designs, echoing the foreign contingent's equally deadening judgement of 'witty' and 'fun'. The sets were *spassosi*, the lights were *spassosi*, the costumes were *spassosi*. They weren't, they were gruesome, but for some extraordinary reason that defies analysis they worked. *In* that setting, *for* that evening, and despite a dozen indications to the contrary, such as that they were glaring, trashy, ugly, badly made, ill suited to the sophisticated and unsophisticated elements of our public alike, they worked. The lighting was livid, bald and aggressive, reminiscent of one of those dreadful rock concerts you see on television. The punk theme was unhappy, managing to be both eccentric and unoriginal at the same time. The costumes were indescribable, clashed badly with the hairstyles and make-up (on which I imagine Joanna was unable to leave her stamp but not for want of trying), and gave off a funny burning smell. The boots were absurd and squeaked. When the stage lit up at the close of the overture to reveal Leporello, resting his elbow on a scrap-heap, attired like a downmarket zombie who's been run over by a tank, even though there was scant space for it to sink to, my heart sank.

And then, for no identifiable reason, to the notes of his opening ditty, slowly, slowly, step by step, beat by beat, up it started to climb again until it achieved an altitude . . . oh, several degrees higher than its original level, I would say, several, several. So high in fact that by the end it had to plummet down again, poor overtaxed organ. Not much credit to me – my choices as director were inspired in pretty well every case by the wrong motives – but the production was a success on a scale I had never envisaged. An oxymoronic success: a huge little triumph, a perfect jewel of no value whatsoever, or vice versa an extremely valuable trinket.

Is that all I'm good for? Throwing off baubles? Am I what's called a lightweight? Is Percy Flage my godfather? Was it he who came to my christening, sprinkling his pernicious snuff over all the other gifts? And if I am a lightweight, why for the sake of blazes don't I have a lightweight's aims to match?

Joanna. Joanna is not for me. Joanna is best left where she is, in the warehouse of my memory theatre, stowed away in her casket with the sun and the swifts and the rest of the props. I can say this now almost without regret, so true I know it to be. At present I see no faults in her, none whatever, but if I turn on her the same merciless eyeglass I use for Gaia I can already see little hypothetical buds where one day the faults might bloom. Her forthrightness, for example, her democratic spirit: how long before these qualities – for qualities they are – would start to jar on me? That dowdy little village woman she sat next to during the performance – oh, very praiseworthy, I don't doubt, backbone of Italy, salt of the Umbrian earth – but not a suitable partner, surely, for an intense aesthetic rally, which is what Joanna seemed to be trying to sustain with her when I approached them. No snobbism in this question, just cultural perplexity. There was a theatre critic in the audience, practised, competent, a friend of Adele Klein's: wouldn't he have hit the ball back harder? Wouldn't I? But, no, it was backhand, forehand, drop shot, volley with

Italy's equivalent to Mrs Archer. Not even a very pleasant creature either – gave me a filthy look when I drew near and turned her broad bucolic back. Manners, those would represent another stumbling block: Joanna clearly places little weight on them; to me they are of Aristotelian importance.

I am a poor vain fish. Gaia understands this and caters for it. Joanna is of another ilk. Far be it from me to defend an arch enemy, but I see that old randy Rubirosa may just possibly have his reasons for seeking blandishment elsewhere. Gaia smelt of tuberoses last night (no, that's not right, the name comes to me from assonance – but anyway of deliciously scented flowers of some breed or other), and as he sat next to her his connoisseur nostrils expanded in rapt reaction: *Sento odor di femmina.* Joanna smelt of turps. It plucked at my heart strings – but again, how long before I started fishing for my handkerchief or reaching out for a mask?

Love? Perhaps after all I have the answer. Perhaps it is simply knowing that better exists but choosing – for all sorts of niggardly little reasons that in the end add up to something rather fine – to stay put.

'And that represents the *summa* of your wisdom on the subject, Henry?'

Who's that talking? Ah, it's you, Plato, and you, Sappho, and you, Dante, and you, Will, and all the rest of the gang. Er . . . yes, I think so, I think, yes . . . that's more or less it.

'Well, poor fish indeed, no wonder you're not much of a writer.'

You asked for that, Henry. Take it on board and get on with it.

*AMABILE – FINALE

That *was* a lovely evening. I needn't have worried about opera being above my head – even Beppe stayed awake for the first half and enjoyed it. Television evens things out for you, I suppose that's what it is; the colours, the faces, the expressions – goes over them with a flat iron; chooses for you what you have to look at too. Live, there's so much more to catch the eye. Shame about what Giovanna went and did to those costumes, because material like that costs money and they'll only be good for dusters now, but she was right, with the coloured lights on they did look rather special – made you think of witches or astronauts or something, at least they did me. I suppose you can't do theatre with an eye on the purse strings. It's the same with all celebrations: you want to put the everyday rules aside and blow everything on just the one do, just the one evening. They didn't teach us that in school, nor at home neither, but I think it's true and sometimes you must forget the cost and step out of the everyday world – buy yourself a ticket to the stars.

That's what it felt like to me, sitting there with those nice old-fashioned tunes playing, and all those pretty lights and shiny surfaces, and the actors' faces – some familiar, some not – and their gestures, and the clever way they mimed the singing and sort of made you understand the spoken bits as well, even though they were said in a foreign language. (The old lady would have liked it – more her days than mine –

but I'm glad in the end she plumped for the telly, or I'd have spent half the time taking her backwards and forwards to the lav.) Yes, that's what it felt like: as if you'd opened up a door and stepped out into dreamland.

I was in a good mood already of course on account of Lucia. The Avvocato's done a wonder there, God bless him. (I wanted to thank him after the show, but he was busy talking to someone on his mobile phone and I didn't like to interrupt: lawyers work long hours too.) And then I was pleased for Giovanna, because she's got her man back again and behaving nicely from the looks of things, and because Vicky's coming back too in a few days' time. And I was pleased for myself because Beppe wasn't fidgeting and because I'd dumped the boys safely and was rid of them for a while, and because – oh, well, because everything in my life seems to be settling back into place again. And about time too.

I found myself, while the show was on, not forgetting about Stefano exactly – which always leaves me with a bad feeling afterwards, as if I'd deserted him – but forgetting to notice whether I was forgetting or remembering or which, seeing as the memories just came and went naturally, without hurting. I had a little pang when Federico walked on stage – he's so like him, and with that false moustache and his hair tied back he could have been his double. And I had one, too, when I saw the Contessa – I don't know why, it's silly of me really, but I just can't get over this idea there was some special kind of feeling between her and Stefano. Both so young and so nice-looking – and all those long journeys together to the airport and places. Nothing there shouldn't have been, of course, nothing improper, but I like to think of some woman his own age carrying a little torch for him in a corner of her heart: Lucia forgot so quick.

And that Conte, he must lead her a bit of dance too, worse than the Avvocato. All that telephoning to Giovanna, all that making up to her, when he's lucky at his age to have the wife he's got. Paola's friend from the bar was quite sly about it: Been in here a few times, she said, the Conte and your Signora. Get on well together, don't they? Very close, very pally, that's nice. But then of course they've got a lot in common, like nationality and the show and . . .

I didn't rise to it, I knew it'd only sound worse if I tried to stand up for her, so I said nothing, just nodded, very cool and casual. But after we'd sat down in our places again and Giovanna was filling me in about the story and other little things I'd missed, I saw him – the Conte – sidling over, making straight for where we were sitting. And at the same time, two places further down, I saw Paola's friend prick up those prying ears of hers and nudge her husband in the ribs, and the injustice of it made me so angry I turned my back on the Conte on purpose (I've never done that to anyone before in my life and it took some nerve) and started gabbling so fast to Giovanna I kind of side-tracked her attention completely. I *will* not have her gossiped about, I *will* not have people saying ill of her, or even thinking it. It's not right.

She's done so much for me one way and another, it's the least I can do in return – protect her reputation. Gave me a picture tonight as well, put it in the car for me to take home. Says it's a portrait of me, but I can't say I can see the likeness myself. Still, it's the thought that counts. What I'm to do with it poses a bit of a problem: the bedroom has that nice matching furniture that I chose myself, and I don't think somehow it would suit; if I leave it in the sitting room the boys will end up using it for dart practice; if I move it to where the old lady sleeps she'll say it gives her indigestion or nightmares. The stairs I suppose are the best bet, on the corner, where it's dark. And when Giovanna comes to visit I'll move it to where Padre Pio is now: I wouldn't hurt her feelings for the world.

It's funny, I was thinking about Padre Pio when the music was on. About miracles and things, and the afterlife, and believing in God. I don't know why, but the music just made my thoughts turn that way. And do you know what conclusion I came to? I must tell Giovanna, I think it'll make her laugh. I thought to myself, well, there can't be a heaven, there can't be, because if there was, then God wouldn't have bothered to make this world so beautiful, the way he has, and fill it with so many lovely things, like colours and music and sunshine and people to be fond of, it'd have been a waste of his time. That's what I thought.

*ORSO MARIA — DA CAPO

Hello? Cristina? This is a message from Orso, Orso Volpi. Do you remember? We met at the opening of the Domus Aurea earlier this summer. You were speaking to a group of visitors about gold-leaf technique in Imperial times, and those beautiful eyes of yours were hidden behind a huge pair of glasses, making you look so intellectual, and I was listening to you, fascinated. You promised to come out to dinner with me one day to tell me more. Would you do that, I wonder? It would make me so happy. I'll call again later, but if in the meantime you want to get in touch with me my number is 0348 774 4903. Best to give just two little rings first, so that I know that it is you and not some boring business call. *A presto. Ciao.*

A NOTE ON THE TYPE

The text of this book is set in Linotype Sabon, named after the type founder, Jacques Sabon. It was designed by Jan Tschichold and jointly developed by Linotype, Monotype and Stempel, in response to a need for a typeface to be available in identical form for mechanical hot metal composition and hand composition using foundry type. Tschichold based his design for Sabon roman on a fount engraved by Garamond, and Sabon italic on a fount by Granjon. It was first used in 1966 and has proved an enduring modern classic.